LILA
AND
HADLEY

All rights reserved. Published by Scholastic Press, an imprint of Scholastic Inc., *Publishers since 1920*. SCHOLASTIC, SCHOLASTIC PRESS, and associated logos are trademarks and/or registered trademarks of Scholastic Inc.

The publisher does not have any control over and does not assume any responsibility for author or third-party websites or their content.

Library of Congress Cataloging-in-Publication Data
Names: Keplinger, Kody, author.
Title: Lila and Hadley / Kody Keplinger.
Description: First edition. | New York: Scholastic Press, 2020. |
  Audience: Ages 9–11. | Audience: Grades 4–6. | Summary: Hadley is an
  angry girl: angry at her mother for embezzling money, angry at her
  estranged older sister, Beth, whom she has to live with while her mother
  is in jail, angry at having to move to Kentucky away from her friends,
  and angry at the world because she has retinitis pigmentosa and is
  slowly going blind; but then she meets Lila, a rescued pit bull who has
  not responded to anyone else—so if Hadley can train Lila, maybe the dog
  can get adopted into her forever home, and just maybe Lila can help
  Hadley deal with her own problems.
Identifiers: LCCN 2019023518 (print) | LCCN 2019023519 (ebook) |
  ISBN 9781338306095 (hardcover) | ISBN 9781338306118 (ebk)
Subjects: LCSH: Pit bull terriers—Juvenile fiction. | Dogs—Training—Juvenile fiction. |
  Retinitis pigmentosa—Juvenile fiction. | Blind children—Juvenile fiction. |
  Sisters—Juvenile fiction. | Mothers and daughters—Juvenile fiction. | Anger—Juvenile
  fiction. | Kentucky—Juvenile fiction. | CYAC: Pit bull terriers—Fiction. |
  Dogs—Training—Fiction. | Retinitis pigmentosa—Fiction. | Blind—Fiction. |
  People with disabilities—Fiction. | Sisters—Fiction. | Mothers and daughters—Fiction. |
  Anger—Fiction. | Kentucky—Fiction.
Classification: LCC PZ7.K439 Li 2020 (print) | LCC PZ7.K439 (ebook) | DDC
  813.6 [Fic]—dc23

10 9 8 7 6 5 4 3 2 1   20 21 22 23 24

Printed in the U.S.A. 23
First edition, April 2020

Book design by Baily Crawford

For Corey,

the dog that changed my life

Chapter One

"I really ain't a dog person."

Mama always says I shouldn't say *ain't*. Says it's not proper grammar. But then, she's also the one who taught me that stealing is wrong, and now that's what she's in jail for. So as far as I'm concerned, she don't got a leg to stand on.

"Did you hear me?" I ask Beth as she puts her tiny car into park and shuts off the engine. "I said I ain't a dog person."

"That's all right. You don't have to touch the dogs. Don't even have to look at them if you don't want. We'll only be here for a few minutes."

"Then let me stay in the car."

"No way. It's ninety degrees!"

"You got air-conditioning."

Beth shakes her head. "Out of the car, Baby Sister. You're

coming inside. But I promise, it won't take me long. Then we can go back home."

"Hadley."

"What?"

"My name ain't Baby Sister. It's Hadley."

I don't gotta look at Beth to know I've hurt her feelings. But I don't care. She's got no right to call me her sister. Not after the way she left us five years back. Three days ago, when she picked me up from Mama's house, was the first time I'd seen her since I was seven and she was nineteen. We might share blood, but we sure ain't family.

"Okay, Hadley," she says, her voice quiet. I hear the click as she unbuckles her seat belt. "Let's just go inside."

"But I ain't a dog person."

She ignores me this time and climbs out of the car. For a second, I think about staying put. It's not like she can drag me out of the car if I don't wanna move. Not without making a real big scene.

But June in Kentucky sure ain't nothing to sneeze at, and Beth's already turned off the car and taken the keys with her. My not wanting to melt into the scorching, cracked fake-leather seat wins out over my not wanting to go inside.

"Do you need my arm?" Beth asks as I slam the passenger-side door as hard as I can. "Can you see all right?"

"I'm fine," I snap. But as soon as the words leave my mouth, my foot collides with the edge of the curb. I start to fall forward, and Beth grabs hold of my elbow and keeps me upright. Once I've got my balance again, I yank away from her. "I said I'm fine."

Beth huffs out a breath, but she don't argue. "All right. Come on, then."

I follow close behind her, keeping my eyes down so I can watch for bumps or steps I might miss as we make our way down the sidewalk and onto a path that leads to a large brick building. When I'm looking right at something, I can mostly see all right. But it's the edges where I get tripped up. Anything out to the sides or below or above a certain point is just . . . gone. It's not darkness or black spots or anything. It's like my brain tries to fill in what ought to be there, so sometimes I think I can see but . . . I can't. And those edges have been creeping in slowly for years. The doctors say I'm already what they call "legally blind." And one day that tunnel of clear vision will be more like a pinprick.

I don't like to think about that if I can help it.

Beth reaches the big front door, and I can already hear

a bunch of dogs barking inside before she's even pulled it open. She gestures for me to walk in ahead of her. I do, but I keep my arms crossed tight over my chest so she knows I ain't happy about being here.

Beth walks to the front desk. There's a tall teenage girl with a round, pale face sitting behind it, talking to an older, bearded man who's clutching a fluffy white dog in his arms.

"Thank you so much, Angela," the man says. "Sprinkles is going to have a good home with me."

"I'm sure she will, Mr. Xu," Angela says. "Be sure to post lots of pictures and tag Right Choice Rescue on social media, okay? We love seeing how our dogs do in their forever homes."

"I certainly will. Or, well . . . my granddaughter will. She says I'm bad at taking pictures." He laughs, says goodbye to Angela at the desk, and leaves, his sandals squeaking against the tile. "Let's go, Sprinkles," I hear him say before he's out the door. He's using that squished, goofy voice people use when they talk to pets. "We have to go buy you some new toys, yes we do."

Beth steps up to the desk then. "Hurray for a successful adoption!"

"Thanks to you," Angela replies, tucking her short red

hair behind her ear. "You worked miracles getting Sprinkles housebroken."

"Some dogs are a little more stubborn than others," Beth says. "You just have to be patient . . . and have the right dog treats." She glances over at me, still standing several feet back. "Angela, this is my little sister, Hadley. She's going to be living with me for a while."

"Oh, hi there," Angela says, voice bright and friendly.

All I do is shrug.

"Is Vanessa in her office?" Beth asks.

"She should be."

"Great. Thanks, Angela."

Beth walks back over to me as the door opens and a couple comes in pushing a stroller, heading straight for Angela's desk.

"I've just gotta go back to Vanessa's office and pick up my check," Beth tells me. "Then look in on a few of the dogs. You can either stay here or walk around if you want. I'll come find you when I'm done, okay?"

Shrug.

Beth sighs again. I make her sigh an awful lot.

I stand there for a while after she walks off, but eventually watching Angela chatting with the couple—who seem very particular about the kind of dog they wanna adopt—gets real boring. So I decide I might as well walk around.

To the left of the desk there's a door that opens onto a hallway. I walk down it until I reach an intersection and head right. A second later, I find myself in a large room full of dog pens. The pens are pretty big, too, giving the dogs lots of room to walk around inside. I must've wandered into the large dog section, I realize, because all the dogs I pass seem huge.

There are dogs in every shape and color. Pointy ears, floppy ears. Dogs with curly hair and dogs with sleek straight fur. Black dogs, white dogs, yellow, spotted. Most of them come to the edge of their pens as I pass, wagging their tails all excited, like I'm here to see them. A few even jump up, paws on the bars, barking. Not scary barking, but like they want my attention.

I walk past all of them.

It's not that I dislike dogs. They're fine, I guess. But we never had one, so I don't get all worked up about them the way a lot of people seem to. I ain't got a clue where Beth gets her love of them from, but she likes them enough that she became a dog trainer. I wonder if she was a dog person when she lived with Mama and me or if that happened after she left us.

I walk past pen after pen, ignoring the dogs inside, until something makes me stop.

I'm standing next to one of the kennels, but the dog inside ain't up at the edge, trying to get me to notice it like the others. Nope. For a minute, I don't see a dog at all, and I think this one might be empty. But then I lower my eyes and see a large brown-and-white lump on the floor. It'd been just outside my range of vision before.

It's a pretty big dog. Real broad and stocky-looking, with high set, smallish ears that flop down at the tips. And its head is huge, flat with a big jaw. Its face is mostly white but with a big brown spot covering most of the left side. I don't know dog breeds real well, but I think I've seen dogs like this on TV. Pit bull, I'm pretty sure.

The dog's just lying there, eyes open, and all I can think is that it looks like how I'd look if I were a dog. Downright miserable. Like it'd rather be anywhere else.

I don't know what makes me do it—I sure didn't plan to—but I find myself crouching down in front of the kennel. And then I'm talking to the dog.

"Hey," I say.

It doesn't move, but I think its eyes are looking my way.

"Bad day?" I ask, as if the dog can answer. And I don't

know, maybe it kinda does. Its face certainly looks like it's saying, "Yes. Terrible day." I nod at it. "Me, too. A whole lot of them lately."

Slowly, I reach my hand through the bars. I know Beth would probably tell me this ain't safe—I don't know this dog or what its temper is like—but I do it anyway. I move my fingers in a beckoning gesture. For a minute, I don't think the dog's gonna come to me. Not like I blame it. I didn't wanna move from my bed today, either.

It takes a second to make up its mind, but it starts to stand. It moves toward me real slow, as if second-guessing every step. I ain't sure what comes over me, but I hear myself cooing to it, softly saying, "Good dog. There we go. Come on." And silly as it might be, it works.

The dog reaches me at last. It stares at my face for a minute. Its eyes are real big and brown and . . . *sad*. That's the only way I know how to describe them. Sad and maybe . . . lonely? Then it lowers its huge head to sniff my palm. Once it's done checking me out, I reach up and scratch behind one of its ears.

And then we both let out this sigh. Right at the same time. Like whatever has just happened has lifted a weight. Like we're both relieved.

That's how I meet Lila.

Chapter Two

When Mama first told me I'd have to go live with Beth, I thought she was pulling my leg. Until she started crying, that is.

Things had been weird for the past year or so. First, Mama had stopped working as Dr. Parker's bookkeeper and gotten a new job cleaning houses, though she wouldn't tell me why. She'd been working for Dr. Parker for years, taking care of all the billing and keeping track of the money for his practice. So I kinda figured something was up when she wasn't working for him no more. Then she was always on the phone with people, and when she'd hang up, she'd be all upset and teary-eyed. When I asked who she was talking to, she told me it was a lawyer, but she said I didn't need to worry about it. She started being real forgetful, never remembering when parent-teacher conferences were, or forgetting to go to the grocery store when we ran out of milk or toilet paper or stuff like that. I'd press her about it sometimes, but she just said she was stressed out and that everything was gonna be fine.

"Don't worry, Bean," she'd say, stroking the back of my head. "It's nothing for you to get upset over. It'll all be okay."

Turns out, my mama is a liar.

She'd lied to Dr. Parker for months while she was stealing money from him, and she'd lied to me every time she said things would be fine. They weren't fine at all. The judge had found her guilty in May, and she was going to jail for a whole year, and now she was telling me I had to go live with my stupid older sister who I hadn't even seen since I was seven.

"I'm sorry, Hadley," Mama said, her voice muffled by the trembling hands pressed against her face. "I'm so, so sorry. But . . . but you'll be okay, I promise. I— Hadley?"

I'd already stormed off. And I made sure to slam my bedroom door real hard, too. She'd lied to me so much. Why should I believe her promises now?

I wasn't just mad about what she'd done or about having

to live with stupid Beth. It was all of it. I'd just finished sixth grade, and I was gonna have to switch schools come August. Beth lived in Kentucky, but I'd spent my whole life in Tennessee. Mama kept saying it was only a three- or four-hour drive, but that's a long way. Far enough that I didn't know when I'd see my friends again after I left.

So no, I wasn't gonna be fine.

I refused to talk to Mama for the next two days, even as she helped me pack up my room. Once Beth came to get me and Mama went to jail to serve her sentence, this house wouldn't be ours anymore. We were just renters, and that meant our landlady, Mrs. Martindale, would be letting new people move in. My bedroom would be someone else's bedroom. And I'd be living in a new state, in a new house, going to a new school . . .

And it was all Mama's fault.

She tried to trick me into talking to her. She made my favorite dinner—pulled pork sandwiches—and offered to let me stay up late to watch TV, but I didn't have nothing to say to her. And when Beth showed up in her little blue car to take me away, I walked out the front door without even saying goodbye.

"Hadley," Mama had called, and I could hear her voice breaking. She was about to cry again. Just like she'd done the day before. And the day before that. "Bean, please . . ."

Beth glanced at me. She hadn't said a whole lot since she'd gotten there. But she asked, "Don't you wanna say goodbye?"

"No."

I also didn't wanna hear Beth's opinion on any of it. She didn't have a right to talk to me about saying goodbye. She hadn't said goodbye to me when she'd left us. One day she'd been there, teaching me how to do a French braid and painting my toenails in the bright blues and purples that Mama hated. And the next she'd just been gone. Walked out on us. So who was she to talk about goodbyes?

"But you know Mama won't be back for a while."

"I don't care," I snapped.

Beth looked over at Mama then. It must've been the first time they'd really looked at each other since Beth left us all those years before. But Mama just shook her head. I went and climbed into Beth's car, slamming the passenger-side door, while she and Mama exchanged a few quiet words. Then Beth got into the driver seat next to me.

"You ready to go?" she asked.

I didn't answer. What did Beth want me to say? Of course I wasn't ready. I didn't wanna go anywhere. I didn't wanna live with her. I didn't want any of this. Mama had spent years teaching me the difference between right and wrong, and now she was the one who'd done something real wrong, and I was being punished, too. It wasn't fair.

Beth started the engine, but before she pulled out, there was a tap on my window. Mama stood outside, gesturing for me to roll the window down.

I didn't move, so after a minute, Beth rolled it down for me.

"Hadley," Mama said. Yep. She was crying. I wanna say it didn't make me feel bad for her. But it did, just a little.

Mama had never been much of a crier before all this. In fact, I'd only seen her cry three times before she stopped working for Dr. Parker. The first time was at Grammy Lora's funeral, when I was four. The second was two years later, the night the police officer showed up to tell her that Daddy had been in a car accident and wasn't coming home. And then, of course, the day Beth moved out.

But she'd been crying an awful lot over the past few months, and especially in the two days since she'd told me the judge's decision. He'd given her a few days to "get her affairs in order"—whatever that meant—before she'd have to go to jail. That's where she'd be spending the next year because of what she did. And as much as I wanted to punish her, too, seeing her hurt still hurt me a little bit.

"Hadley," she said again, reaching through the open window to squeeze my shoulder. "I love you, Bean. You know that, right? No matter what happens, I love you so much. And I'm sorry. But I'll see you soon, okay? I'll write to you. And Beth can bring you to see me . . . Right, Beth?"

"Sure," Beth said. "Any time Hadley wants me to bring her for visitation, I will."

"You hear that, Bean?"

I didn't answer.

Mama swallowed hard. "Okay. Well . . . be careful. Take care of yourself. I love you."

"I'll take care of her, Mama," Beth said. "I promise, she'll be fine."

That's when I decided Beth was probably a liar, too.

I was angry and heartbroken and scared. I didn't know if I'd ever be "fine" again.

Beth and I finally pulled away. And even though I didn't want to, I caught myself staring in the side mirror, watching

Mama still standing in the driveway, hands over her face, until I couldn't see her no more.

Which, I guess, didn't really take all that long.

"So," Beth said after about an hour of driving. She'd been talking basically nonstop. Just "trying to fill the silence" as Mama would have said. Talking about her job as a dog trainer and her clients and also the dog rescue she'd been working with and the house she lived in and the school where I'd be going in August. Talk, talk, talk. But then her voice had turned a bit nervous. "Mama told me your eyes have been getting worse. Because of the . . . shoot. What was it called again? RP stands for . . . uh . . ."

"Retinitis pigmentosa," I muttered. I hated those two words. They sounded harsh and ugly, and I'd heard them a million times in the past couple years. Usually by eye doctors who said it in that serious I-have-bad-news voice.

"That's it," Beth said. "Thank you. Anyway, I was talking to Mama about it, and I got to thinking, maybe it's about time you start making some preparations. For when it gets worse, you know? Mama said she'd been meaning to look into different programs or classes that could help you, but with everything going on she hadn't had a chance. So I did some research, and we could get you a teacher. Someone to show you how to walk with a cane and cross streets safely. That kind of thing. We might even be able to find you a Braille teacher if that was something you'd be interested in. What do you think?"

"I don't need a teacher."

"Oh."

"I can get around fine. I can see *fine*."

"Well, sure, maybe for now," Beth said as she switched on the windshield wipers. It had started raining. Because the day wasn't awful enough, I guess. "But, Hadley, it's going to get worse, and it can't hurt to be prepared. Learning some new things might even be fun. You might make new friends."

"Not interested."

"Okay," she said, with a tone that told me I was clearly testing her patience. "I'm not going to make you do anything you don't want. But it's something to think about. I just . . . I wanna be helpful."

I didn't respond. I didn't want to think about it. I didn't want her bringing it up, either. What did she know about how much I could see or what was good for me? Nothing. She didn't know nothing.

That sure didn't stop her from trying, though. We'd gotten to her house that afternoon, and I'd pretty much been shut up in her guest bedroom ever since.

She'd tried to get me to unpack.

"It'll make you feel more at home, Hadley."

She'd tried to get me to eat more.

"You'll feel better with a full stomach, Hadley."

She'd tried to get me to go outside and help her with her flower garden.

"We could all use some fresh air sometimes, Hadley."

It's been two weeks, and my stupid sister refuses to just leave me alone. All I wanna do is stay in bed watching YouTube videos on my phone, texting my friends back in Tennessee, and eating potato chips. But instead, she insists on dragging me all over this new town with her.

"It's okay to be angry and upset," she told me a few days ago. "You've got every right to be. But this isn't healthy, Hadley. I'm worried about you. We gotta find something— something you enjoy. Something that'll help you cope with being here."

I ain't so sure Lila is exactly what she meant.

Chapter
Three

"Well, this sure is a surprise."

I jump, startled by the voice behind me, and snatch my
hand away from the dog I'm petting. It seems startled, too,
but probably more because of my sudden movement than
anything, and it scurries back, moving toward the other end
of its kennel.

I turn around to see who's rude enough to come up and
scare me like that, and I find myself looking up at a tall,
pretty black woman, who I guess to be in her midtwenties,
around the same age as Beth. She's dressed in a short-sleeved,
navy-blue button-down shirt and khaki shorts, and her dark,
curly hair is pulled back. She smiles down at me, all warm and
friendly like. "Sorry," she says. "Didn't mean to startle you."

"Well, you did," I snap, folding my arms tight over my chest.

"How'd you get Lila to come to you?"

"Who?"

She nods to the kennel at my back. "The dog. How'd you get her to come over and let you pet her?"

I shrug. "Dunno. I held my hand out and she just . . . came over. Why? What's it matter?"

"Interesting." The woman steps closer, looking past me and into the pen. "I've never seen her do that before. Lila's been here for months, and most days we can barely get her to look at us, let alone come to us."

Slowly, I turn around to look back into the kennel. Lila has retreated into the corner, where she's already curled up, facing the wall, sure enough. "I didn't do anything special," I say. "Promise."

"You must just have the magic touch," she says, smiling at me again. "What's your name, by the way? Are you one of the youth volunteers? I haven't seen you before."

I shake my head. "Uh-uh. My name's Hadley. I'm—"

"Oh!" the woman says, and her smile gets even bigger, if that's possible. "You're Beth's sister. That explains it."

"Explains what?"

But before she can answer, there's the sound of a heavy door creaking open and thudding closed, and Beth's voice echoes over the sound of barking dogs as she calls out, "Hadley? You in here? We can go ahead and go. I can't find . . ." She trails off just as her footsteps round the corner, into the main strip of kennels where the tall woman and I are standing. "Oh, Vanessa, there you are. I was looking for you."

"Well, you found me," the tall woman—Vanessa, I suppose—says, and now she turns that big smile on Beth.

Beth giggles. It's a nervous, quiet giggle, and she ducks her head away. I can't quite tell from this distance, but I'd wager her cheeks are burning pink, too.

"Looks like your sister inherited your skill with dogs," Vanessa tells Beth.

Beth clears her throat before replying. "That so? Hadley told me she wasn't a dog person."

"I'm not," I mutter.

"Could've fooled me," Vanessa says. "She got Lila to come to her. I watched it happen. Lila walked right up to the edge of the kennel and let Hadley pet her."

"Are you serious?" Beth starts moving toward us now, toward Lila's kennel. Inside, the pit bull still ain't moved. It's like she's trying real hard to ignore us. Can't say I blame her.

I know it ain't fun, hearing people talk about you like that, like you're not even there. Beth doesn't seem all too concerned about this, though. "You're sure? Lila? How?"

"Positive. And no idea how. I asked, but Hadley says she . . . held out a hand. Lila must just like her more than the rest of us."

"She must," Beth murmurs. "You ought to be flattered, Hadley. Lila doesn't seem to like anybody." She puts a hand on my shoulder, giving it a little squeeze, but I jerk away and put a big step between us.

"It ain't a big deal," I say. "It's just a dog."

There's a long pause, where nobody speaks, and even the other dogs' barking seems to quiet a little bit. Finally, though, Vanessa says, "Hadley?"

I look over my shoulder at her. "What?"

"Forgive me. I wasn't being very polite. I didn't introduce myself. I'm Vanessa Truchet. I run Right Choice Rescue."

"Yeah. Kinda figured."

"Hadley," Beth hisses. "Don't be rude."

But Vanessa just keeps beaming at me. Does this woman ever *not* smile? I feel like smiling so big like that would make my cheeks hurt. "I might be overstepping here," she says, "but I have an idea. I think you should take Lila."

"What?!"

The word pops out of Beth's and my mouths at the same time—with the same sound of disbelief.

"Vanessa," Beth says, "you know I can't adopt a dog right now. I'm already so busy with work. And now with Hadley here, money is going to be tight. I can't afford a new dog."

"Not *adopt* Lila," Vanessa clarifies. "Foster her."

"Foster?" I ask.

"Yes," Vanessa says. "Lila would come home with you and Beth, but it's just temporary. The rescue will keep paying for all her food and medical expenses, if they come up. Except she'll get to live with you, and you can train her."

"Train her?" Vanessa has to be out of her mind. "I ain't got a clue how to train dogs."

"Lucky for you, you've got a sister who's real good at it."

"I don't know, Vanessa," Beth says. "I've been working on training Lila since she got here, and she's not responsive. Just because she came to Hadley one time doesn't necessarily mean anything."

"You might be right," Vanessa admits. "But that's more interest than she's shown in any of us in months. And if Lila does like Hadley, she's got a better shot at breaking through than we do. If Hadley can get her trained, socialized a bit, then maybe we can even get Lila adopted. She's clearly miserable here. But we can't adopt her out until she's got at least basic training and is a little friendlier. Besides . . ." I watch her make eye contact with Beth. "It'll give Hadley a nice project for the summer."

I hate the way they look at each other, that meaningful pause that passes between them. It makes it real clear they've been talking about me. Beth has probably told Vanessa all about how she can hardly get me to leave my room most days. How I'm mean and angry, and how she's worried about me and my health, or whatever.

And now Vanessa is in on it, too. Trying to fix me when I don't wanna be fixed.

"You might . . . have a point," Beth says.

"Y'all gotta be kidding me," I snap. "Beth, I keep telling you, I ain't a dog person! I don't wanna do this."

Even as I say the words, though, I catch myself turning to look at Lila again. And I can't shake that feeling I had when I first saw her. That pull that got me to crouch down and offer my hand. Maybe I ain't a dog person, but it sure sounds like Lila ain't a people dog, neither. For some reason, though, we'd reached out to each other.

And apparently that's enough for Vanessa and Beth, who are already talking out the details and hunting down a crate for us to take Lila home in. They walk off, telling me they'll be back in a few minutes. I sigh and sit down on the concrete floor, looking through the kennel's bars at Lila.

"Can you believe this?" I ask her.

She shifts a little, moving so she ain't facing the wall no more but instead has her head half turned in my direction.

"Looks like we're gonna be stuck together. I warn you, I don't think I'm real good company these days, but . . . at least you won't be here, I guess."

Lila takes a breath and lets it out like a sigh.

"Yeah, that's how I feel," I tell her. "Oh well. I guess we can be miserable together."

Ten minutes later, Vanessa and Beth are loading Lila's crate into the back seat of the little car. They'd made me lure her into the box because she wouldn't respond to either of them. And even with me, she hadn't seemed too willing. But they'd given me treats, and I'd managed to coax her inside. Vanessa helps Beth lift the heavy box and scoot it across the seat before shutting the back door.

"We can give it a couple weeks," she tells Beth and me.

"If it seems like it won't work, at least we'll know. But I think this might be the perfect solution for everybody."

"We'll see," Beth says. "I'm still a bit skeptical. But if it can give Hadley a nice project and . . ."

I grunt and storm off, tired of hearing them talk about me. I climb into the passenger seat and slam the door. Through the window, I can see them still chatting for a minute. Then Vanessa gives Beth a quick hug and heads back inside.

Beth just stands there for a minute, watching her go, before walking to the driver's door and getting into the car. "Well," she says, "this sure isn't how I expected today to go."

I ignore her and instead stare out my own window.

Beth sighs. "All right. Hadley, Lila . . . let's go home."

Chapter Four

"I already told you no."

I put my hand on Lila's furry white chest and push. Her front paws, which had been on the edge of the bed, slide backward, and she lowers herself to the ground with a little huff of annoyance.

"Don't blame me," I say, flopping onto the pillows. "Beth's the one who says you ain't allowed on the furniture."

Lila gives a quiet whine and puts her head on the mattress, ears tucked back and big eyes staring at me. It's like she knows how pathetic she can look, and that I ain't blind enough yet to resist.

"Oh, all right," I say, scooting over a bit to make room as Lila clambers up onto the bed next to me. "But if Beth asks, it ain't my fault. Not that she ought to care. She says I gotta make myself at home here, and if that's the case, this is my bed now. She don't get a say if you get up here or not."

Lila drops her chin onto the pillow next to my head. She doesn't look at me anymore, though. Just stares at the wall. She does that a lot, I've noticed. Since we brought her here a few days ago, she ain't done much besides lay around the house, staring at nothing, looking sad. Which is pretty much what I do, too, I guess. So at least I have company for it.

I reach out and start to stroke the back of her head and neck. She don't really respond when I do this, but she lets me. Not Beth, though. Any time she's tried to touch Lila, the dog's turned and scurried off in another direction. Not like she's scared of her. More like she just don't want a thing to do with her. I think Vanessa was right. I should feel flattered Lila likes me. Even if I ain't sure why she does.

My phone buzzes, and I gotta root around beneath the covers to find it. When I do, I see it's a notification—my friend Joey has tagged me in a picture he posted. He and my other best friend, Maya, are in Gatlinburg. Joey's parents take an overnight trip there every summer and always let Joey bring along two friends.

I'm supposed to be there right now.

babykangaroo42: Me and @MayaFairLady about to go shopping in Gatlinburg! So glad I saved up my birthday money. Wish you were here, @Hadleybean13. We miss you!

I know I ought to type a response—tell them to have fun, tell them I miss them, too—but instead I just push my phone away and bury my face in the pillow.

I ain't talked to Joey or Maya since I left Tennessee. When I told them I was moving away and wouldn't be there all summer—or even be starting school with them again in August—they'd wanted to know why. And, truth is, I was way too embarrassed to tell them the real reason. It was bad enough I knew what Mama had done. I didn't want them knowing, either.

So I'd told them Mama got a new job and we were moving to be closer to my sister. And I hadn't elaborated any more than that.

They've been texting me almost every day. And sometimes I'll reply with a smiley face or a heart emoji or something. Just enough so they don't think I'm ignoring them but so I don't gotta answer, either.

I miss them a whole lot, and I'm still mad as a hornet

that I ain't with them right now. But I feel like talking to them will just make me feel worse. Because they'll ask me all kinds of questions—about my new town and if I've made any friends or where I'll be going to school. And I don't wanna tell them the truth. That I'm miserable and scared. That seeing their pictures just makes me sad. That I'm worried I won't make any new friends. Or that, even when Mama gets out of jail, I ain't sure what will happen. Because we don't have our house anymore. And I don't trust Mama now. And everything is gonna be different and . . .

I bite down on my lip and squeeze my eyes shut. I ain't gonna cry. Nope. Not gonna think about any of that anymore.

Through the wall, I hear the front door open and Beth's muffled voice as she chats with Mrs. McGraw, the annoying older lady next door who's been staying here with me while Beth's at work. Even though I'm twelve and really don't need a babysitter.

I still don't have a real grasp on Beth's work schedule. She always leaves around nine in the morning, but some days she's home by midafternoon and others she ain't back until nearly dinnertime. I don't bother asking her about it, though. I don't want her to think I'm interested.

A second later, I hear the front door close again and Beth

hollers, "Hadley, I'm back from work! I bought takeout for dinner."

I don't answer. I don't gotta. I know she'll just walk on in here. Beth, I've learned, ain't much of a knocker.

Sure enough, I hear the doorknob jiggle, and my older sister steps into the guest room she's been calling mine since I arrived. She stands in the doorway for a second, then sighs real loud.

"I thought I said she couldn't get on the furniture."

"I told her that," I say, my voice still muffled by the pillow. Reluctantly, I roll over so I can look at Beth. "But she didn't listen. Besides, it's my bed. She can be up here if she wants."

"She didn't listen because she's not trained," Beth reminds me. "Which is what you're supposed to be working on. Have you even been out of bed today, Hadley?"

"Yeah. Of course I have."

It's true. Kinda. I did get out of bed a couple times. Once when Mrs. McGraw knocked on the door about half an hour after Beth left for work. I'd intended to let her inside and then go straight back to bed, but Mrs. McGraw insisted on making me breakfast, telling me I was too skinny and asking me a million questions about how I was liking my new neighborhood.

Lila had stayed in my room the whole time. I was

jealous. It was easy to be antisocial when you had four legs and couldn't speak. I'd gone back to bed after eating, though, so she didn't get my room to herself for long.

The other times I'd gotten up were to take Lila out into Beth's backyard so she could do her business. I thought that'd be a little harder—talking her into peeing outside—but she did it right away. If I bothered with this training thing, at least housebreaking her would be easy. Even if it did mean picking up her poo with a plastic bag. Ick.

Beth clucks her tongue like she don't believe me, but she changes the subject. "You got a letter in the mail today." She reaches into her purse and pulls out something small and white. "It's from Mama." She takes a step closer to the bed, stretching her arm out, making to hand me the envelope.

I don't take it, though.

After a long moment, she lowers her hand. "Do you want me to read it to you? I don't know how well you can see to read—"

"I can read fine," I snap, even though that ain't exactly true. I can read—I've just gotten real slow. My field of vision has gotten narrow enough that I can only focus on one or two words at a time. Meaning it takes me forever to read even a page. But I'm sure as heck not telling Beth that.

"Oh . . . Sorry. I wasn't sure."

"I just don't wanna read it," I say. "Throw it out."

"Hadley . . ."

"And when she calls tonight, I don't wanna talk to her then, either. Or ever. So don't bother asking."

"Hadley."

"What?" I demand. My voice is getting too loud, because Lila lets out a grumble before climbing off the bed and moving to the corner of the room. "I don't gotta read it if I don't want. And you can't make me talk to her. You ain't one to judge anyway. You don't even like Mama."

"That's not true."

"You didn't talk to her for years," I remind her. "We hadn't seen you since you left home. If you can just go like that, leave us for good, then I can ignore a letter and a phone call if I want to."

Beth doesn't say anything for a long moment, then quietly moves toward the little desk across the room, placing the envelope on it. She sits down in the chair but turns so she's still looking at me.

"I know you're angry," she says, voice soft. "I know you don't want to be here. And I can't say I blame you. What Mama did . . . it wasn't right. And you've got every right to be upset with her. But she does love you. A lot. Be as angry as you need to be, but don't forget that, okay? And that's all I'll say on that for now."

"Good," I mutter.

But another minute passes, and Beth still ain't left the room. I sigh, loud and pointed, but it doesn't budge her from the chair. Only now she's looking over at Lila, curled up in the corner.

"Have you started reading any of the dog training books I left out for you?" she asks.

"No."

"Why not?"

"I don't want to."

"Why? Because you ain't a dog person?" she asks. "You keep saying that, but then I come home and find you all cuddled up with Lila."

"She got on the bed. I told her not to."

"Uh-huh." Beth sounds like she's about to laugh, which just aggravates me.

"I never said I wanted to train her. That was all you and your girlfriend's idea."

"She's not my girlfriend," Beth says, real quick. She pauses then. "I mean . . . why would you think Vanessa's my girlfriend?"

"You want her to be," I say. "I may be a kid, but I ain't clueless."

She groans. "My God. I'm so obvious even a twelve-year-old can tell I like her. Bet that means Vanessa knows, too."

"She definitely knows."

"Okay, okay. That's not the point here." Beth clears her throat. "We're talking about Lila." She shakes her head. "I can't make you train her if you don't want to. But if you're not going to even try, I have to take her back to the rescue."

"Fine," I say, pulling the blankets over my head. I want to stop talking.

"Is it?"

The mattress sinks, and Beth pulls the blanket off my face. I glare at her.

"Hadley . . . Lila can't stay at Right Choice forever," she explains. "There's only so much room there. If we can't adopt her out, then we'll have to find her somewhere else, so we can make room for dogs we can find homes for."

"Somewhere else?" I ask, even though I don't think I want her to answer.

"A shelter, probably," Beth says. "They take in dogs from different places—dogs they think they can work with—and try to adopt them out. With Lila, she was at a shelter in another town. I think she'd been moved around a bit. But Vanessa pulled her out of the shelter and brought her to Right Choice. Lila's never been aggressive, just distant. Vanessa thought Lila would be easier to work with in our setting, where she'd get more time and attention, but unfortunately . . . well. Anyway. The rescue doesn't have a lot of space. And keeping Lila there, when they can't find her a home, means one less kennel they can give to a dog we *can* find a home for. Do you understand what I'm saying?"

"What's so bad about a shelter?"

"Nothing, necessarily," she says. "Some animal shelters are no-kill shelters. Meaning dogs and cats can live there as long as they need. They're not that much different from the rescue Vanessa runs. But . . . those are often already overcrowded. I can't promise that's where Lila would end up, even though they'd try very hard to get her into one if they can't keep her."

I don't need to ask her what the other shelters are like. If some shelters have to specify that they're no-kill, then . . . The reality of what she's saying makes my stomach hurt.

"That's why Vanessa was so excited when she saw Lila letting you pet her," Beth tells me. "We've been trying to train her since she came in. But she won't respond to me or any of the volunteers. Barely lets us touch her. No one is going to adopt her if they can't even pet her, especially if she isn't trained. You're the first real hope we've had for her. I'm not saying that to make you feel bad or pressure you if you really don't wanna do this." She sighs. "Honestly, it's a ridiculous idea anyway. But Vanessa seems to think that between Lila's liking for you and my experience training dogs, we might make something work. I hope she's right. But if you don't want to do it, I can't force you."

I look over at Lila, still lying in the corner. She's watching me now, though. Eyeing the bed like she's just waiting for Beth to leave so she can reclaim her rightful spot.

Beth might not have said it in so many words, but I know what she's trying to tell me.

I'm Lila's only hope.

But I can barely stand to be around people myself these days. How am I supposed to train this dog and get her to be friendlier? It kind of feels like we both need some training, if you ask me.

"Just . . . keep all that in mind, okay? You never know. Y'all might end up having fun. There's a dog park a block from here. Maybe y'all could go there? You'll wanna do some leash training with her, but it could be good for you both. Even just getting out of the house to take a walk around the neighborhood together. Or practicing with her in the backyard?"

I don't say anything.

"Fine," Beth says, with an irritated sigh. The mattress shifts again, and she stands up and moves toward the door. "If you're hungry, I brought home KFC. Sorry. Too tired to cook tonight. But you'll have to come in the kitchen to eat it. I'm not serving you dinner in bed."

My stomach grumbles at the thought of fried chicken. And loud enough I can't even pretend I ain't hungry.

"I'll be in there in a minute," I mumble.

"Good."

She's already back in the hallway before I call out to her. "Beth?"

Her blonde head pokes back into the room. "Hm?"

I sit up slowly, pushing the blankets off. I'm still in my pajamas. I ain't changed all day, but Beth doesn't seem surprised by this.

"About Lila," I tell her, glancing back over at the pit bull again. "I'll . . . I'll think about it. Training her, I mean. I'll think about it."

Chapter Five

The next day, I actually roll out of bed and put some clothes on. I ain't doing it for Beth—though she's been trying to coax me into getting out of the house for days. Nope. I'm doing it because I know Mrs. McGraw will be here any minute, and I'm gonna need an excuse to get away, or else she'll want to talk to me for an hour.

"Come on, Lila," I say, grabbing the leash Beth had hung on the hook by the door. I haven't used it on Lila yet. Beth says she's only slightly leash trained, and I've mostly been letting her out into the backyard to pee. But if I gotta leave the house now, so does she.

She don't come to me right away. She just lifts her head from where she's lying on the living room floor, stares at me for a minute, then looks away.

"Nice try." I march over to her and hook the leash to her collar. "Now come on." I give the leash a tug. She don't move. I sigh. "Do you wanna be stuck here with Mrs. McGraw when she comes over? If I ain't here for her to pester, she's gonna focus on you."

Logically, I know Lila can't understand what I'm saying, but it sure seems like she does. Because that gets her to her feet.

"Good girl."

Sure enough, when we're halfway to the door, there's a knock, and Mrs. McGraw's voice calls through the door, "Hadley! It's Mrs. McGraw! I brought you some leftover casserole."

I pull open the door with a grimace. I don't understand why grown-ups always bring casserole to other people's houses when, really, I don't think anyone actually likes it. Luckily, it's barely ten in the morning and I've had breakfast, so I got an excuse not to eat the stuff.

"Hi, Mrs. McGraw," I say. She's already stepping past me and the dog and making her way to the kitchen. "Lila and I are going for a walk. We can't stick around to chat right now."

"Oh, that's lovely," Mrs. McGraw says. "I'll just put this

in the fridge then. Maybe Beth can heat it up for y'all for dinner." I hear the refrigerator door open and shut, and then Mrs. McGraw is walking back into the living room. She wipes her hands on the thighs of her oversized denim overalls before adjusting her steel-gray bun. "I'll come with you on that walk."

"Um . . . no. That's okay." I'm trying real hard not to snap at her. But the idea of her coming with us, hovering over us, talking at us . . . I wanna get out of the house to avoid talking, not to do more of it. "Lila and I are just gonna go on our own."

"Well, I don't know, Hadley," Mrs. McGraw says, and now she's using that gentle, concerned voice I hate. "I ain't so sure that's safe. Beth told me about your sight and all. I'd feel better if I went with you."

"I don't care how you feel." The words leave my mouth before I can stop them, but I can't really say I feel bad, either. "I'm not five, and I can see fine. I'm just walking the dog around the stupid block. I don't need you or want you coming with us."

I ain't real good at seeing facial expressions most of the time, but even I can see the shock on Mrs. McGraw's face.

Her jaw drops open and she lets out a little gasp. "Well, my word," she says. "Hadley, that is an awful ugly way to talk to somebody. I have half a mind to tell your sister."

"Go ahead," I mutter. "Let's go, Lila."

I tug the dog out the door with me, and she follows, leaving Mrs. McGraw in Beth's living room. Beth's gonna be real mad at me when she gets home. But I don't care. What's she gonna do? Ground me? Make me go to my room? Those are rewards, not punishments.

My old house was out in the country. We never really had neighbors. Not any within a mile or two, at least. We were surrounded by cornfields on all sides, and you had to drive to get just about anywhere. Beth's neighborhood is different, though. She lives in what I figure must be a "suburb." I've heard that word used on TV, and while the houses here seem smaller than the ones on the shows I've watched, the rest seems pretty similar. The yards ain't too small, but they ain't big either. And lots of them are surrounded by wooden or metal fences.

"Keep up," I tell Lila as I try and move her down the driveway and to the sidewalk. But Beth was right, she's not real good on the leash.

When I wanna go left, she tugs right. Half the time she

42

walks so slow I feel like we're crawling along, and the other half she goes so fast I think she's gonna pull my arm off. Then there's all the stopping to sniff the ground. Sometimes she stops so suddenly that I end up being jerked backward because of her. I guess that's one of the things I'm supposed to be training her on, though, huh?

There ain't a lot of people out here—it's midday in the summer, and it's blazing hot. Anyone who ain't at work is probably sticking close to their air-conditioning. Good. I like it better that way, with it being just me and Lila. Empty sidewalks, no one smiling at me or trying to chat. And I figure Lila feels the same.

Despite what I told Mrs. McGraw, I do gotta be a little careful as I walk. I hate to admit it, but my eyes have gotten bad enough that I can't really see the ground when I'm looking straight ahead anymore. I gotta keep looking down at the sidewalk, keeping an eye out for roots that have warped the concrete or big cracks that might cause me to trip. And even then, I get smacked in the face by a few low-hanging branches a couple times.

When my hair gets caught in one branch, I have to stop and untangle it. Lila stands next to me, looking up at me with eyes I'm gonna assume are full of judgment.

"This ain't my fault," I tell her as I yank my hair free. "Who has trees this close to the sidewalk? My being able to see ain't got nothing to do with it."

A second later, we round a corner, and I can hear voices and a few barking dogs. Lila and I both stop, and I turn my head to see what looks to be a large, fenced-in lot across the street. I can't make out much of what's going on over there, but I suddenly remember Beth telling me there was a dog park about a block from her house.

Big, booming barks and tiny, shrill yips are carried my way by the summer breeze, along with laughter. Kids' laughter. Probably kids off school, like me, walking their pets. Just like me.

Next to me, Lila is staring at the dog park, too. Only she's letting out this little growl while she does.

"You don't wanna go over there, do you?" I ask.

Lila stops growling and looks up at me. She whines.

"Yeah. Me neither," I tell her.

But we both stay put, just standing on the sidewalk, watching (or, in my case, mostly listening to) the people and animals in the little park.

I hear the creak and slam of the gate before I notice the girl. She's just stepped out of the dog park and is crossing the street toward Lila and me, a large, fluffy black dog in tow. I can't make out any details of her face, but I can tell she's kinda short with wavy, dark brown pigtails. And when she calls out to me, she sounds like she's probably pretty close to my age.

"Hi!" She's about halfway across the street now, moving toward us. And her voice is real chipper. All excited and upbeat in a way that makes me take a step back. "Cute dog you got there! Y'all heading to the park?"

I shake my head. She's getting closer, almost to us now. And Lila's started to whine, tugging on her leash in the opposite direction. "No . . . No, we're just . . . walking."

"I ain't seen you before," the girl says. She's on the curb now, right near me. And her dog's got its tail wagging like crazy. "You just move here or something?"

Now that she's close, I can see that she's got a real big smile on, all her white teeth showing. It makes my stomach flip over. She wants to talk to me, to ask questions. She's gonna ask about why I'm here, about Mama, about why I can't see good. And I don't wanna talk about any of that. Not to this strange, smiling girl. Not to Beth or my friends back in Tennessee. Not to anybody.

"Sorry, I gotta go."

"Oh, all right. See ya later!"

I turn and start to move back around the corner, Lila dragging me along after her at top speed. She seems even more desperate to get away from the happy girl than I am. She pulls harder and harder, moving me faster. Too fast for my eyes to keep track of all the things I know I gotta watch out for. Everything blurs past us. I yank at Lila's leash, trying to get her to slow down, but she don't. She's too far gone now, practically running down the sidewalk, like she's done forgot I'm even attached to her.

Then my toe catches on a tree root that's pushing up through the sidewalk. I hadn't seen it coming, and I'm moving too fast to catch myself. For a split second, I'm airborne, both feet off the ground, before I land—hard—on my chest, sliding a foot or so across the concrete. I feel the skin scrape off my knees just as Lila's leash jerks out of my hand. Lila keeps running, like she ain't even noticed what's just happened, and all I can do is push myself up, into a kneeling position, as I try and catch my breath.

The first thing I think is, *I hope that girl didn't see.* But when I look over my shoulder, the sidewalk behind me is empty. The girl must've gone the other way.

But now I'm really alone, and I can't see Lila no more, and suddenly that's what's got me panicked. I clamber to my feet, knees aching, and start walking down the sidewalk, calling her name. I gotta watch my feet to keep from falling again, which is hard because I still wanna keep my eyes up as I hunt for the dang dog.

"Lila?" I yell. "Lila, come here, girl!"

But it's pointless. I know, from everything Beth's told me, that Lila ain't gonna come when called. She ain't trained. That's supposed to be my job. And I've barely worked on it at all. So now there's an unhappy, untrained dog on the loose, and it's all my fault.

My heart's pounding, and my feet stumble as I try to walk faster, hoping to catch up to wherever she's gone.

"Lila!" I call out again, even more desperate this time.

What if something happens to her? The image of Lila running away from a stranger and right into the street flashes in my mind. My stomach drops. If she gets hurt, it'll be all my fault.

I keep walking, circling the block once and then twice, calling and calling for her. I even stop and ask a few people on the street if they've seen a pit bull with a leash dragging behind her, but no one has. Enough time has passed that she could be anywhere in this neighborhood by now. This neighborhood I ain't familiar with at all.

And when I'm trying to look for her, I can't keep my eyes on the ground. So I keep tripping over uneven bits of sidewalk or running into people's trash bins that haven't been pushed out far enough. Which only makes me even more frustrated and upset.

When my phone buzzes in my pocket, I have a foolish moment of thinking maybe someone is messaging me about Lila. Even though that don't make a lick of sense. Lila's collar has the phone number and address of Right Choice Rescue. If anybody found her, they wouldn't be contacting me.

Still, I feel a pang of disappointment when I realize it's just a notification. My friends have posted another picture and tagged me in the caption. It's a photo of Joey and Maya, their faces pressed together so they can both fit into the selfie. They're grinning from ear to ear. Joey's red hair is long and falling over his face, and Maya's big, dark brown eyes are magnified by her thick black-rimmed glasses. They look so goofy and happy.

MayaFairLady: We're leaving Gatlinburg this morning. Had a great time with @babykangaroo42. Wish you'd been here with us, @Hadleybean13. Miss you! XOXO.

I shove my phone back in my pocket, irrationally angry that they'd tag me in that *right now*, when I'm in the middle of trying to find Lila. I know that's silly. Ain't as if they know what's going on. But still. I wish they'd just stop tagging me altogether. All it does is remind me that I'm *not* there. That my face ain't squished between theirs in that selfie. That even if they miss me, they're still having a good time without me, while I'm miserable.

I take another walk around the block before giving up. I'm not gonna find her. I'm gonna have to explain to Mrs. McGraw why I'm coming back with scraped knees and no dog. And she'll call Beth . . .

Beth's gonna be so mad at me.

That thought makes me more upset than I imagined it would.

My feet drag and I choke back tears as I make my way back to Beth's house. My stomach hurts and there's this heaviness in my chest. I'm going over and over in my head what I'm gonna say to Mrs. McGraw and then to Beth. But then I reach the front steps and still, none of it sounds right.

Just as I'm walking up to the door, I hear a quiet little bark. It's like the dog version of someone saying *psst*. I freeze on the top step and look around, but I still don't see nothing. Then I hear it again, coming from right beneath me.

I stumble down the steps and crouch, looking under the little porch. It takes me a minute to spot her—it's kinda dark in there—but sure enough, I see Lila lying in the dirt, staring back at me. I hold out my hand and she gets up, walking toward me with her head down, like she knows she's done wrong.

"I ain't mad," I tell her. My voice cracks on the words as I grab hold of her leash. I wrap it around my wrist, an extra bit of security just in case. "Not at you, anyway. Come here."

I take a seat on the steps, and Lila flops down at my feet. I can feel tears starting to slip down my face. I was only barely holding them back before, and the sense of relief after that stress makes the dam break. Still, I can't shake the sensation of a heavy weight on my chest.

"You scared me, you know," I tell her. "If you hadn't come back here . . ."

Lila looks up at me, then lowers her head again, covering her face with one paw.

"It ain't all your fault. You shouldn't have run like that, but . . . if I hadn't fell . . ."

If I'd had a cane . . .

I hate the thought, mostly because I know it's true. Mama's brought up the idea of me learning to use a cane a few times over the past year or so. And now that I'm here, Beth keeps bringing up the idea of orientation and mobility lessons. I've been saying no to the idea for so long, telling myself I'm all right, that I can see well enough to get by without any help. But if I'd had a cane today, I might have noticed that tree root. I might've been able to stop and hold on to Lila's leash.

I reach down and scratch Lila behind the ears. I don't say nothing else for a while, but I think she knows exactly what I'm thinking.

Things are gonna have to change.

The front door swings open behind me, and Mrs. McGraw's gravelly voice exclaims, "There you are! I was getting worried. Had half a mind to come looking for you."

"We weren't gone that long," I mutter, keeping my head down so she can't see that I've been crying.

"Maybe not," Mrs. McGraw replies, "but after the way you left . . . Well, never mind that now. Come on in. You can have some casserole for lunch."

"Fine." Slowly, I stand up and turn toward the door.

"Oh, Hadley!" Mrs. McGraw gasps. "Are those scraped knees? Did you fall? Bless your heart. Come on inside so we can get those cleaned up."

I make eye contact with Lila. She looks about as tired as I feel. After a second, we both head inside. Even if things do gotta change, everything that happened today can stay our secret.

Chapter Six

The doctors first told me I was losing my sight a couple years ago, but apparently it'd been happening for a while before that. It happened real slow, so I didn't hardly notice.

I remember walking out of the grocery store with Mama one night in the winter. The sun had set, and the lights in the parking lot had come on. But as Mama walked toward the car, pushing the grocery cart and expecting me to walk behind her, it hit me all of a sudden: I couldn't see.

I could see the headlights from cars pulling in and the glow of streetlamps, sure, but they just looked like bright, gleaming spots surrounded by darkness. The lights were just little orbs of contrast, but they didn't actually light up anything around them for me. Later, the doctors would explain this had something to do with how retinitis pigmentosa affects the rods and cones of my eyes or something like that, but at the time, all I knew was that I used to be able to see in situations like this, and then I just couldn't. And I hadn't been able to for a while.

It wasn't scary. Not really. Because my vision hadn't gone away all at once. It was more that I noticed the change all at once, even though it'd been going on for a long time. Like, standing on the edge of that parking lot, I realized that a year or two before, I'd been able to see in places like this, even when it was dark. And the change had happened so gradually, I didn't have a clue when I'd stopped being able to see.

The same thing was happening with space at the edges of my vision. I was having to turn my head more and more to see things out to the sides and stumbling over things I should've been able to see without looking down.

So Mama took me to the eye doctor, who sent me to a fancier eye doctor, who ran all sorts of tests before telling me I was going blind. I wasn't legally blind just yet, but I would be soon, and it would just keep getting worse from there.

At first, I really didn't know what *legally blind* meant. But as far as I understand, it basically just means my eyes are bad enough that, as far as the government or laws or whatever are concerned, I might as well be blind. Even though I can still see some. According to my doctor, most blind people actually do have some vision. It just ain't a whole lot.

"You know, Bean," Mama said one night last autumn. "I've been thinking about something."

We were walking out of the movie theater after seeing the newest Pixar movie. Back then, Mama liked to have Girls' Night once a month, where we'd go to a movie or out for dinner or spend a couple hours at the mall together. Just the two of us.

"Hmm?" The movie theater had been dark, and it was dark outside now, too, so I was holding on to Mama's arm as she led the way to the car.

"Well," Mama said, "with how things are going with your vision, I was thinking it might be a good idea to start looking into . . . I don't know. Some classes maybe? Like you could learn to read Braille. Or maybe we can find someone to teach you how to cook? The kinda things that might be hard once your eyes get worse. And I could look into you getting one of those white canes. I don't know a lot about it, but I could find out. I'm sure your school could work with me."

"Meh. I don't need any of that," I said.

"That so?"

"Yeah. I mean, I don't need Braille because I can still read all right. And I don't gotta learn to cook because you do that for me."

Mama gave me a playful bop on the back of the head when I said that.

I grinned up at her, even though I couldn't see her face too well in this lighting. "It's true!" I insisted. "And as for the cane—I get around fine."

"Bean, you can't see real well *right now*," Mama pointed out.

"That's just because it's dark," I said. "I'm fine during the day, and I ain't got no reason to go anywhere by myself at night."

"Don't say *ain't*, Hadley." Mama stopped next to the passenger side of the car and opened the door for me. Once I was inside, she shut the door before going around to her own seat and hopping in next to me. "Seat belt, please," she said, then continued with what we'd been talking about a second ago. "And I know you don't go anywhere by yourself at night right now. But someday you're gonna want to. You'll be in high school, and you're not gonna want to hold on to your mama's arm."

"Sure I will," I said. "I won't ever be embarrassed of you, Mama."

"I find that hard to believe," she said. She started the engine, but she didn't back out of the parking spot yet. "I'm being serious, Hadley. I think . . . some sort of classes, just to make sure you're prepared, could be good. I'm gonna do my best to teach you everything I can, but . . . but this is new for me, too, Bean. I've never been blind, and I'm not sure how to teach you everything."

I sighed. "I'm okay, Mama. You can teach me fine. Do we gotta talk about this?"

"I'm afraid so, Bean." She reached over and stroked the back of my head, her fingers sliding through my hair. "Why are you so resistant to this?"

"I dunno," I mumbled. "I just . . . I guess I wouldn't mind learning to cook or something. But I don't wanna use a cane. People will think it's weird and they'll laugh at me."

"What people?"

"People people," I said. "People at school. My friends . . ."

"Do you really think Joey or Maya would think you were weird for using a cane if it helped you?"

"No . . . Or maybe? I don't know."

"I don't think they would, Bean," Mama assured me. "And if they did, they aren't the kinda friends you deserve."

"Even if they don't, other people will."

"Oh, Hadley." Mama sighed as she leaned across the center console and wrapped her arm around my shoulders. "I wish I could tell you nobody will be jerks and laugh or say mean things. But I can't promise that. What I can promise you is that the people who do laugh are the ones with the problem, not you. And they won't be worth a bit of your time."

I shrugged, because I knew she was right, that those people would just be jerks, but I wasn't sure that mattered. Who cared who'd be laughing at me if there were people laughing at all?

"I can also tell you that if it's being laughed at that you're worried about, *a lot* more people would laugh at you for having your mama around in high school or college than if you used a cane," she said. But now there was a note of teasing in her voice. "I'm sure glad you aren't embarrassed of me. I love that you're still willing to hold my hand in public. But you won't always want me next to you. And I'm not always gonna be able to be there. And I want to know that you're still safe when I'm not there."

"I guess."

"I'll tell you what," she said, pulling away from me and leaning back into her own seat. "We don't have to do anything right away. But I'll start looking into classes and stuff—figure out how it all works—and then we can talk about it again. Maybe we get a good start on this when you're in seventh grade? That way you'll have all sorts of time to get set for high school. You'll be able to go out with your friends without me tagging along. And hey, if you learn Braille, you could teach Maya and Joey, and y'all could send little coded messages."

"Maybe," I said.

"If that's as close to a yes as I'm getting for now, I'll take it," she said as we pulled out of the movie theater parking lot. "We'll put this on hold for the moment. In the meantime, how does some ice cream sound? I'm feeling like a trip to Dairy Queen is in order."

Truth was, the idea of starting high school using a cane sounded awful. But I knew Mama had a point. Still, I didn't want to deal with it right then. I wanted to put it off as long as possible.

And, without knowing it, I got my wish. It wasn't long after that that the calls from the lawyers started and Mama got all distant and upset. She didn't look into those classes. Or, if she did, she forgot to talk to me about it. And I tried to forget, too. To pretend I didn't need any of it.

Even though she'd been right. She wasn't always gonna be there to hold my hand.

She isn't here right now, after all.

Chapter
Seven

When Beth gets home that night, after my disastrous walk with Lila, I come out of my room to talk to her. She's real surprised by this, I can tell. She don't do a good job hiding it from her voice.

"Oh, Hadley!" she says, looking up from the pot she's stirring at the stove. "Are you hungry? Sorry it's taking me a bit to get dinner going. It was a long day. And I'm not used to making food for two people just yet."

"I ain't hungry," I tell her. "I mean, I could eat, but that ain't what I wanna talk to you about."

"Oh." Beth finishes stirring the pot, then leaves it to simmer before coming over to sit at the tiny table. "Why don't you sit down. What is it you need to talk about?"

I don't sit. "It ain't a big deal," I tell her real quick. "Don't make it a big deal."

"Make what a big deal?"

I sigh. "That thing you talked about. That . . . that movement training, or whatever it was called. To help me get around better because of my . . . because my eyes are getting . . . you know what I'm talking about."

"Orientation and mobility," she says calmly. "It would help you as your vision gets worse. What about it?"

"Right, that." I catch myself chewing on the inside of my cheek and force myself to quit. "Um . . . could you get me signed up or something? So I could . . . start classes or . . . training or whatever it's called."

"Of course," she says. She sounds even more surprised now. "I thought you weren't interested. What made you change your mind?"

I shrug. I sure as heck ain't gonna tell her I fell and lost Lila today. She'd get all freaked out and lecture me, probably, or ask me if I'm okay a hundred times. I'm wearing my long pajama pants right now, even though it's hot, so she can't see my scraped knees. Mrs. McGraw probably told her about them, but I don't wanna remind her and risk any questions. "I dunno. I just figure . . . it's boring around here. Might as well have something to do."

"Hmm."

She don't believe me. Before she can ask any more questions, though, I say, "Also can you buy some baby carrots?"

"Baby carrots?"

I nod. "Not for me. I don't like carrots. But they were in that salad Mrs. McGraw brought over the other day. I gave mine to Lila and she really liked them. More than she's liked the dog treats you brought from work."

Beth sighs. "Hadley, you're supposed to be training her. Not giving her table food."

"I know, I know." I wave my hand. "But it ain't table food if the carrots are just for her. And . . . and if she likes them so much, it might help me train her. It's worth a try, ain't it?"

"Hmm. Well. If she does like them more than the dog treats, then . . . sure. I'll pick some up." She goes to check the pot on the stove before she asks a question. "So have you thought more about it, then? Are you going to try and train her?"

"I . . ." I'm chewing on my cheek again. "Maybe. Yeah. I guess." I shrug. "I started looking stuff up on the computer this afternoon. There are a lot of YouTube videos about dog training. Watching those is easier for me than reading a bunch."

"I hadn't even thought of that." She turns off the stove and starts opening up cabinets, grabbing dishes and utensils. "Videos being easier for you, I mean. It's a good idea. Do you need help finding more? I can do some digging and—"

"I got it," I snap. I don't mean to. I know she ain't doing anything wrong, really. But she's just so eager to help all the time, and it makes me feel kinda bad. Like she don't think I can do anything on my own.

"Okay, okay," Beth says. And now she sounds irritated, too. Clearly I'm trying her patience real hard. "Dinner will be done in just a second, but how about after, I can maybe show you a few things that might help? We can do a bit of training with Lila together."

"Sure," I mutter. "I guess."

Mama calls right after dinner. As she does every night. And, as I do every night, I refuse to talk to her. So while Beth spends fifteen real awkward minutes talking to her—catching her up on her own life—I wash the dishes, grab Lila, and head into the living room to wait. When my sister is off the phone, she comes to join us, a bag of dog treats in her hand.

"We'll have to wait on the baby carrots," she says. "These will do for now, though. First, make sure she knows you have them. Give Lila a treat so she knows what she's working for."

I take one of the treats from Beth and offer it to Lila. She sniffs it for a long moment before taking it. And nearly swallowing it whole.

"Careful," I tell her. "You're gonna choke on one of them if you keep that up."

Lila just tilts her head at me, like she's expecting more.

"Good," Beth says. "Now she knows what she's working for. Let's start with teaching her to come when called. That's a pretty simple one."

But it sure doesn't seem simple. Every time I try, Beth tells me I'm not doing it right.

"Lila, come?"

"A little firmer," she says. "Not a question. You gotta let her know you're in charge."

"Lila, come!"

"Not so harsh," she says. "You don't wanna scare her."

"Lila, come."

"Louder."

"Lila, come."

"Softer."

And through all of it, Lila doesn't get off her butt and come over to me even once. She just stares at Beth and me, like she thinks we're ridiculous. Even when I hold out the treat to her, trying to lure her over, she just stares at it. Like it ain't enough to convince her, and she don't got a clue why I'm not just bringing it over to where she's waiting.

Eventually, she gets bored with Beth and me. She stands up and walks right out of the living room, back toward my bedroom.

"Ugh!" I throw the dog treat in my hand onto the ground in frustration.

"Calm down," Beth says. But she sounds frustrated, too. Except I'm guessing her issue ain't with Lila. She picks the treat up off the floor before saying, "I'll go get Lila, and we'll try again."

"No."

"What?"

"I don't wanna try again. This ain't working. I'm done."

"Training dogs isn't always easy," she says. "It takes time. Especially with stubborn dogs like Lila. You've got to keep working at it."

"I will, then. But not with you," I snap. "You're just

confusing me more. The people in those YouTube videos are way better teachers than you."

"You are being so rude right now," Beth snaps back. "I'm just trying to help, Hadley."

"I don't want your help."

"Fine, then!" She drops the bag of dog treats onto the coffee table. "Figure it all out yourself."

"I will."

"Whatever, Hadley."

She walks away from me then. She sits down on the couch and grabs the remote. I watch her for a second, but she ain't looking at me. I know I ought to apologize. I know I've been rude, even though she was trying to be patient with me. But the more patient she acted, the more irritated I got. And I just couldn't stop myself from pushing those buttons.

It's obvious that living with me right now ain't easy. I've overheard Beth, on nights when she thinks I'm asleep, talking on the phone with her friends. About how she's having to watch her budget more because she's got an extra person to take care of now. About how she can't go on any girls' weekend trips because she's gotta be here for me. About how she feels like she can't say anything right around me. She ain't said anything mean, just . . . that things are hard.

I've made things hard.

So I know I *ought* to apologize.

But I don't.

Instead, I walk out of the living room in a huff and go back to my room.

Lila's lying on my bed again. She might be getting too spoiled, being allowed up there, though she ain't tried to get on any of the other furniture. Mostly because she hardly leaves my room unless I'm taking her outside. Or, like tonight, Beth and I make her.

I sit down on the mattress next to her. After a second, she lifts her big, boxy head and puts her chin on my knee with a sigh. I reach down and stroke from the top of her head down her back. Again and again.

When I talk to her, it comes out in a whisper.

"We're gonna keep working on all that stuff, you know. Just you and me. But you gotta actually try, okay?"

She closes her eyes for a second, and I imagine she's trying to pretend she's asleep. Like she can't hear me.

"I'm serious, Lila. But . . . if it makes you feel better . . . You ain't the only one who's gotta get some training."

I get a funny image in my mind then. Some faceless lady introducing herself as my mobility instructor, holding up a leash and a book called *How to Train a Blind Girl*. I don't think that's quite how it works, though. Pretty sure. The thought don't quite make me laugh, but it does make me smile a little.

"All right, Lila," I say. "I'll make you a deal."

Might just be my imagination, but I think the dog turns her nose just a little toward me, eyes flicking open as I talk. Whether it's real or not, I pretend she's paying attention.

"I'm gonna actually give this orientation and mobility or whatever—this training thing—I'm gonna give it a try. But if I do it, you gotta work on your training, too, okay?"

Lila doesn't move.

"I mean it," I say. "If I gotta be trained, so do you. If I can't train you, Beth's gonna take you back to the rescue. And I ain't sure you'll ever get adopted. And if they have to send you back to a shelter . . . I don't even wanna think about what might happen to you, okay? So do we got a deal?"

I hold my hand down toward her, like we might shake on it. I don't really expect her to move, of course. So when she does it surprises me.

She doesn't put her paw in my hand or nothing like that.

That'd have been way too impressive. But she does lift her head up off my knee, look at my hand, and bump her nose against it. I'm so surprised by it, I do actually laugh this time.

I'm pretty sure she was just trying to tell me to pet her again, but that's all right. I'll take it.

I grin down at her. First time I've grinned in a while, I think.

"Good enough. Looks like we got a deal then, Lila."

Chapter Eight

"Ah. You must be Hadley. Nice to finally meet you."

It took a few days and a bunch of phone calls, but Beth eventually set up my first orientation and mobility lesson with a lady named Cecilia Labra. On Friday, I say bye to Lila before climbing into Mrs. McGraw's station wagon so she can drive me to the community center for my first class.

The woman who greets me is short—not a whole lot taller than me—with brown skin and wavy black hair that falls to her shoulders. She approaches me with a smile that's so big it makes me wanna hide.

"I'm Cecilia Labra. You can call me Cilia. Or Ms. Labra if that makes you more comfortable. It's up to you." She pauses for a second, standing right in front of me, then says, "Oh, and I'm holding out my hand for you to shake."

"Huh?" I look down, then realize she ain't lying. Her hand is held out to me, and I hadn't even seen it. I feel my cheeks heat up, annoyed and embarrassed, as I grab hold of her hand and give it a quick shake before pulling away.

Cilia just keeps smiling. "Sorry about that," she says. "Your sister mentioned you have retinitis pigmentosa. I should have known better."

She exchanges a few words with Mrs. McGraw before the older lady leaves, promising me she'll be back to pick me up in an hour. Once she's gone, Cilia turns back to me.

"Come on. I'll introduce you to the others."

"Others?"

"That's right. You didn't think you were the only visually impaired person in town, did you? You'll have a few classmates today. We'll do some lessons one-on-one as time goes by, but for your first lesson, I figured it'd be fun to start with some other students around."

"I doubt it," I mutter.

"Hmm?"

"Nothing."

"All right. Well, we're in a room over this way. Is your vision okay in here, or do you want to take my arm?"

"I'm fine."

I follow her through the lobby of the community center and down a short hallway. She stops at a door on the right and pushes it open. "Okay—Addie, Syd—I'm back. And I brought our new student," Cilia says, stepping aside so that I can walk into the well-lit, rectangular room.

I expect to find people my age, but that ain't the case. Instead, there are two kids staring back at me. Young kids. The girl, with her braided yellow pigtails, round, slightly sun-tanned face, and baby-pink romper, looks like she might be in third grade. And the boy, short and scrawny with olive skin and giant glasses on his little face, has to be even younger. They're stopped in the middle of the room, like we walked in on them in the middle of playing a game of tag. In their hands, each is holding a long white cane with a bright red section near the bottom.

"This is Hadley," Cilia tells them, resting one of her hands on my shoulder. "She'll be having her first mobility lesson *ever* today. Isn't that exciting? You two welcome her nicely, okay?"

"Hi, Hadley," the two kids say.

I raise my hand and give them a half-hearted wave, but then I remember—if they're here, that means they gotta be blind, right? Probably blinder than me. So they might not be able to see me wave. Begrudgingly, I sigh and say, "Hello."

"Hadley, am I correct in thinking that you've never used a cane?"

I nod.

"All right. You can take a minute to get to know Addie and Syd, then, while I try and find one the right height for you."

She walks over to a duffel bag in the corner of the room. As she unzips it, I can hear the objects inside clacking and clanging together. I turn and look back at Addie and Syd, but they ain't looking at me anymore. They've started playing again, chasing each other in small circles around the room. Fine by me. What am I supposed to talk about with little kids anyway?

A minute later, Cilia comes back over to me, holding one of those white canes like the kids have. She puts it in my hand and asks me to hold it in front of me so she can see if it's the right height. I do, and the top of it—where the black, rubbery grip is—comes up right to the center of my chest.

"Perfect," she says. "This'll be good for now, and if it turns out you need something a little bit longer, we can do that. Sound good?"

I shrug.

"Okay. First thing's first. Let's show you how to hold it. And then we'll go over some of the different techniques you can use. Addie and Syd—why don't you two come over here and help me demonstrate? Let's show Hadley how we're supposed to hold our canes when we're using them."

The kids quit playing their game and take a few steps toward us before stopping next to each other, each of them positioning their cane in front of themselves. I stare, trying to figure out exactly how they are holding the things so I don't embarrass myself. But before I can strain my eyes too much, Cilia starts explaining.

"What you should do is, hold on to the cane's rubber grip with your right hand. See how one side of the rubber grip is flat and the rest is rounded? On the flat side, extend your pointer finger so it's flat against the grip, pointed toward the ground, and your other fingers wrap around. Yes, like that. I know that feels a little weird, but it'll help you keep control of the motion of the cane once we get to that part," she explains.

I do as she says, or try to. She has to readjust my hand so I get it right.

"Now," she continues once I'm holding it right. "Keep

the tip of the cane on the ground. It should be out, away from your body. The hand holding the grip should stay centered in front of you. Right in front of your belly button. Yes. Just like that. Your hand will pretty much stay right there as you walk. You'll just use your wrist to move the cane back and forth in front of you to find if there are any obstacles coming up. Does that make sense?"

"I guess."

"You'll see what I mean once we get started. Now, who wants to show Hadley the different ways you can use a cane? Addie, you can show her the tapping motion. Syd, why don't you show her the sweeping motion."

"So, for tapping," Addie says, as she begins to walk across the room, her cane clicking along in step. "You just do this."

"Addie," Cilia says, "remember, Hadley can't see well either. Can you explain for her, please?"

"Oh. Okay. Well, you just tap. The cane comes off the ground in the middle, and you tap it on either side of you while you walk. So when you step with your right foot, you tap on the left."

"Why is that?" Cilia asks her.

"So you always know what to expect for your next step.

So if there's something in the way, my cane finds it before I step with my other foot."

"Right. And how far does the cane come off the ground when you pick it up?"

"Only an inch or two."

"That's right. Good job, Addie. You get all that, Hadley?"

"Yeah," I mutter. It all sounds real easy. I don't know why she's making a big deal out of it.

"Syd? Wanna explain sweeping?"

"The cane goes back and forth," the boy says. "But it don't come off the ground."

"That's right. It's a lot like the tapping motion, only the cane tip stays on the ground. Now, some people use sweeping all the time. And some people use tapping all the time. But we learn both. Can you tell me why?"

"Um," Addie says. "Because tapping is easier in, like, sand and snow and when the ground is really bumpy and stuff."

"Right," Cilia says. "Sweeping is great on flat sidewalks or inside. But it can be tricky when you're on uneven ground or in things—like you said—like sand or snow where pushing the cane along on the ground could be hard. Great job, guys. You're helping me teach today."

I can't help but roll my eyes.

This gets boring real quick. Cilia continues going over the different techniques for using a cane—even going into how there are different cane tips that can be more useful for different methods. There are round, rolling ball tips and marshmallow-shaped tips and skinny, pencil-like tips and probably more, too, but I lose track. Then the kids excitedly show off what they know. Cilia makes me do the different motions over and over without actually moving. It's way too easy for someone my age. Obviously. If these little kids know how to do it, I can pick it up real fast.

When Cilia finally does let me try to use the cane while moving, she just has me walking back and forth across the room, with Syd and Addie on either side of me, moving way faster than me, which is annoying. Like using this thing ain't nothing to them. But when I try to keep pace, Cilia starts calling after me, reminding me to keep the cane near my belly button and to make sure I'm moving it in step with my feet so I don't miss anything and not to pick it up so high when I'm using the tapping method.

Okay, so maybe it ain't as easy as I thought.

I'm feeling irritated and embarrassed by the end of the hour, sure these stupid kids are probably laughing at me behind my back for how much Cilia had to correct me. And like it can't actually be as challenging as Cilia makes it out to be—it's just a cane. You move it in front of yourself so you don't run into stuff. It ought to be simple. But with all the rules she's throwing out there, seems like it ain't.

And on top of that, my wrist is kinda sore from doing the motions over and over again.

I'm starting to think I shouldn't have bothered with this at all.

"Looks like our time is up," Cilia says finally. "Nice work today, everybody. Addie and Syd—I promise we'll do some outside practice next week. Thank you for being such good helpers today. Hadley, fold the cane up for me and bring it here so I can put it away."

I stare at her, confused. "You mean I don't get to keep it?"

"Not yet," she says. "I prefer to wait until my students have had a bit more practice before I let them take the cane home."

"But they get to keep theirs," I say, pointing at the little kids.

"They've been taking mobility classes for a while now," she explains. "You'll catch up. Give it a couple more weeks, and the cane will be all yours."

"A couple weeks?" I demand. "That's . . . that's stupid. This ain't even that hard. How much more could I possibly have to learn?"

Cilia sighs. "Language, Hadley. And . . . a lot, actually. Most students I work with take mobility classes for years. It's not just about learning to use a cane, but also how to travel independently. Planning routes, taking public transportation, even navigating things like shopping malls and other places alone. The cane comes into play in all that, of course, but I'm not just here to teach you to use a cane. I'm here to prepare you so that you can take on any situation, even when you can't see."

Years? I might have to take these classes for *years*?

I grit my teeth, fold the cane, and hand it back to her. She smiles at me when she takes it and puts it back into her bag, but all I do is glare. I don't wanna take classes with Cilia for years. I don't wanna be here, in Beth's town, for years.

I don't wanna be going blind at all.

When Mrs. McGraw picks me up and asks me how things went, I don't answer her.

In fact, the only time I talk about the class at all is that night, when I'm lying in bed and Lila hops up onto the mattress.

"I'm only doing this for you, you know," I tell her. "I hope you're grateful. So even if you find me annoying when we're training and stuff, you'd better listen anyway."

Lila just lets out a huff.

"I mean it," I say. "If I gotta put up with this, so do you. And we're getting started for real first thing tomorrow."

Lila snorts and turns her head away from me. I can tell she don't believe me, but that's all right. She'll find out how serious I am soon. And then we'll both get to suffer through our own different types of training together.

Chapter Nine

Despite her attitude, I think Lila may have been listening after all. Or maybe it's just the baby carrots Beth brought home from the store. Either way, she does start making progress.

I remember Beth said that I should start with something simple, so I try and teach her "Come" again. On my own this time.

We practice in my room while Mrs. McGraw watches one of those home makeover shows in the next room. She has a loud, witchy cackle that she lets out whenever one of the hosts says something funny. I'm glad she's entertained enough that she ain't bothering us.

To get started, I let Lila try one of the carrots first, so she can remember how much she likes them. Then I take a few steps away, holding another carrot in my hand. "Lila! Come!"

She sorta just looks at me at first, tilting her head like she's asking "Why?" until I hold out my hand and she sees the carrot. Then she bolts toward me so fast she nearly knocks me over as she snarfs the little orange snack out of my hand.

"Careful!" I scold, even though I'm laughing a little bit. "But . . . yeah, kinda like that. We'll try again."

Teaching her is a whole lot easier without Beth looking over my shoulder, telling me what to do. It only takes the afternoon for Lila to pick it up. Turns out, Lila's real smart. I even get her to start coming to me without bribing her with carrots. I'm beginning to think this whole training thing is gonna be a lot easier than I thought.

I'm so excited by our afternoon's work that I run into the living room as soon as I hear Beth pushing open the front door when she gets back from work. I think I startle both her and Mrs. McGraw, who lets out a surprised gasp when Lila and I barrel into the room.

"Hadley!" Beth says, voice pitched up with surprise. "I'm glad to see you up and about."

"I got something to show you," I tell her. "Lila learned something today."

"Already?" Beth asks.

I nod.

"Okay." She sets down the bags of groceries next to the couch, then smiles at me. "Show me."

"Is that what you've been up to all afternoon? Training the dog?" Mrs. McGraw asks. "Well, that's real nice. Can I watch, too?"

"If you want," I say. Honestly, I'm glad for the audience for once. I can't wait to see how impressed they are with the work Lila and I have put in.

I tell Beth where to stand, making sure there's a decent bit of room between her and Lila, who's lying on the carpet with a paw over her face. Like she's trying to ignore the three people in the room. That's fine. She won't be ignoring us for long.

"All right," I say, hurrying over to sit on the couch with Mrs. McGraw. "Now, Beth, tell her to 'Come.'"

"Okay." Beth clears her throat and puts on her talking-to-dogs voice. "Lila . . . Lila, come!"

Lila don't move. Not an inch. She doesn't even twitch.

"Try again," I say, frowning at the stubborn pit bull across the room.

Beth does, but nothing changes. She even fishes a bone-shaped dog treat from her pocket and holds it out when she calls, but she might as well be invisible for all Lila pays attention to her.

"I'm not so sure she's listening to you, Beth," Mrs. McGraw says with just a touch of amusement in her voice.

I stand up, my hands balling into fists at my sides, and I grit my teeth. "She was doing it earlier, I swear. She was real good at it, too."

"I believe you," Beth says. But that ain't good enough. I don't want her to believe me. I want her to see it herself.

"Stupid dog," I mutter.

"Well, is that language really necessary, young lady?" Mrs. McGraw asks.

I scowl at her.

"It's all right, Hadley," my sister assures me. "Training dogs takes time. And Lila's here because she's proven to be difficult. But the fact that she's listening to you—learning anything from you—proves that Vanessa was right. We made the right call. I've been working with this dog for months and it's always been like this. If you've made any progress today—even just a little bit—that's huge for Lila. She'll get there. Just keep trying."

So I do, but I don't get quite as excited about it after that day.

Over the next two weeks, Lila and I both hold up our end of the bargain. I go to my mobility lessons—where I still ain't allowed to take home my cane—and Lila learns how to "Sit" and even "Stay."

At least, she learns to do it for me. When there ain't nobody else around.

"Why do you gotta be like that?" I ask her one night after another failed attempt to show Beth what I've taught her. This time, I was the one giving the command, Beth was just in the room watching. But when I told Lila to "Sit," she looked over at me, looked over at Beth, then just turned and walked out of the room. I hollered after her to "Come" but she ignored me. And a second later I heard the springs on my bed creak, meaning she'd climbed up for one of her many dog naps.

We're sitting on my bed now, me leaning against the

headboard with my legs folded, her lying at the foot, with her chin resting on her paw. Her eyes are open as she stares at me.

She's got real sad eyes, I think. Maybe that's a silly thing to think about a dog, but I can't help it. There's something about them that just seems *lonely*.

"You wouldn't be so alone if you let people see what you've learned," I tell her. "Some real nice family would probably be happy to adopt you if they saw how smart you are. But you gotta show other people, not just me. Why won't you try?"

She don't answer, of course. But as soon as I ask, I realize she don't need to. Because I understand.

Truth is, I feel awful lonely, too. I know that don't make no sense. Beth's here and is always wanting to spend time together. Mama calls and tries to talk to me every day. Joey and Maya are always texting me, asking how I'm doing, what my new house is like, and Mrs. McGraw tries real hard to make conversation with me or get me to watch TV shows with her when she's here during the day. I've got people who want to be around me. It's me pushing them away. I'm lonely, but trying to do anything to fix it just feels too tiring. So I just keeping ignoring people or, like with Beth, lashing out.

It ain't something I like about myself right now, but it's all I can seem to do these days.

I shift onto my knees and crawl to the foot of my bed, stretching out on my stomach with my head on Lila's back. She turns her face for a second, licking my cheek, before resting her chin on her paws again.

"I guess . . . I guess at least we got each other," I say. "I mean . . . I ain't a dog person. Not at all. But you ain't half bad." I reach up and scratch behind one of her ears as I speak. "I know it's tough. Everything feels tiring or annoying. But the rescue ain't gonna be able to keep you if you don't learn some stuff, Lila."

She picks up her head and turns it away, staring in the opposite direction. Like she don't wanna hear what I've got to say.

"I know, I know." I sigh. "But it's for the best. Do it for me, at least?"

You'd think I'd feel ridiculous, talking to a dog like that, like she could understand a word of what I was saying. But I don't. Talking to Lila feels easier than talking to anyone else. Maybe it's because she don't talk back, don't try to give me advice or comfort me with words that mean nothing. Or maybe it's those sad eyes. I ain't sure.

But I am starting to think she understands more than I give her credit for.

Because on Friday, something changes.

I come home from my fourth mobility lesson, and this time, Cilia lets me take the cane home with me.

"I trust you to be responsible with it," she tells me before Mrs. McGraw picks me up from the community center. "You've done a very good job so far, but I want you to get some practice at home. Use it when you go out with your sister. Next week we're going to start doing some routes outside, now that you've got the hang of using it indoors."

I don't tell her that I hardly ever leave the house, even when Beth asks me to go places with her. Instead, I just nod. My wrist is aching from the repeated motion of using the cane for the past hour, and even though Cilia keeps saying that'll get better once I practice more, I ain't so sure I wanna deal with it.

Still, Beth makes a whole thing out of this, like it's some sort of big accomplishment and not just a stick I get to bring home. She badgers me about what my favorite food is because she wants to make a nice dinner to celebrate.

"It's nothing to get worked up over," I tell her, irritated. "It's just a cane. Little kids get to bring theirs home. It ain't special."

"I'm just proud of you," she says, sounding defeated. "But okay. If you don't want to have a nice dinner, we won't."

"I don't."

She sighs and plops down on the couch. I know I've disappointed her, and I feel a little bad, but I don't know what to do about it.

So instead I look over to Lila, who's lying on the carpet again.

"Lila, come," I say, not thinking much about it. I just wanna pet her. But when she gets up and walks over to me, I hear Beth take in a sharp breath.

I look over at her, confused, but then realize what's just happened.

Beth doesn't say anything, just watches us.

"Lila . . ." I say slowly. She's standing right in front of me, looking me dead in the eye. "Lila . . . sit."

She does.

I look at Beth again, who's got her hands over her mouth.

"Lila . . . stay," I say. I walk away from her, moving toward the doorway. The dog's head swivels to follow my movement. I pause for a minute, then say, "Come."

She stands up and walks to me, walks right past Beth, not at all shy about her being there.

I can't help myself. I grin at my sister.

"Looks like I have both of y'all to be proud of," Beth says.

I reach down and scratch Lila's ears. She gives two quick tail wags, which, for her, is a lot.

It's like she knows. Like she remembers our bargain. She knows I've made progress with my training, so she's got to, too.

"Beth?"

"Yeah?"

"My favorite food . . . it's pulled pork sandwiches. Can . . . can you make that? For dinner tonight?"

I can hear the smile in Beth's voice when she replies. "I think I can manage that."

Chapter Ten

Beth may have been real proud of me for getting to finally bring my cane home, but it ain't long before I wanna throw the dang thing away and never look at it again.

"Ow!" I cry as the top of the cane's rubber grip slams into my stomach, like a tiny—but strong—fist going for my gut. The tip got caught in a crack on the sidewalk, and I wasn't able to stop moving fast enough to avoid the impact. "Crud," I growl, teeth gritted, as I take a step back and shake out my wrist, still holding the cane.

Cilia had scheduled a lesson for me on a Thursday afternoon. It's just the two of us. No Addie and Syd. And that's about the only thing I can be happy about, because at least they ain't here to embarrass me by making everything look easier than it is.

This ain't the first time I've jabbed myself in the stomach with the stupid cane. In the last hour, walking up and down the main street outside the community center, I've probably done it ten times. And based on how tender the area is starting to feel, I can guess that I'll have a ring of bruises right around my belly button later.

"You okay?" Cilia asks, stepping up beside me. She's been spending most of the lesson walking a couple paces behind, calling out directions or advice when she needs to. Now that I know the different cane techniques—sweeping and tapping and whatnot—she wants me to get practice outside, in an environment that she says ain't so predictable.

I think maybe she just wants to torture me.

"No," I snap. With my free hand, I clutch my stomach. All right. Maybe I'm being just a little bit dramatic. But it *does* hurt a lot.

"With a bit of practice, you'll get used to it," she says.

"Used to impaling myself?"

"No." Cilia laughs, but I wasn't being funny. "You'll get used to using the cane. The different techniques. You'll build up your reflexes so you're able to pick up the tip before you walk into the top bit, or shift your wrist so it doesn't hit you. That sort of thing. My students who've been using canes for years all went through this when they first started, and none of them have this problem anymore. Like anything, it just takes time."

She makes me start walking again, this time turning down another street where we pass some local businesses. She walks next to me for a pace or two, reminding me that the arc of my sweep should go just a bit past my shoulders on each side. Then she falls back again, and I walk on, trying to focus on what I'm doing.

I keep the swish of my cane in step with my feet. When I step forward with my right foot, my cane sweeps out to the left, so that I'm always aware of what's just a step ahead. I try not to walk too fast. Maybe if I'm slower I won't slam into my cane next time it gets snagged.

But it ain't long before focusing that hard gets boring, and my mind starts to wander, away from this lesson and back to Beth's house, where Lila's probably waiting for me at the door.

That's what she does when I'm at these lessons, according to Mrs. McGraw. It's the only time I'm away from the house, really, and every time I get back, I find her in the living room, curled up near the door, staring. Like she's waiting for me. I'd be lying if I said it didn't feel kinda nice, knowing she likes me that much. Especially since, truth be told, when I'm away from the house, I miss her, too.

Her training's been going pretty well. She still won't really do things Beth tells her to, but she ain't so shy anymore, either. Beth even wants to bring Vanessa over for dinner soon to show her how much progress Lila's made.

When she mentioned that, she got all nervous and giggly.

I ain't sure exactly what's going on between the two of them right now. But I think maybe Vanessa figured out my sister likes her. Or maybe Beth finally told her. Either way, Mrs. McGraw came over two nights ago to babysit me (even though I told her and Beth both—again—that I don't need babysitting) because Beth had somewhere to go. She left in a dress and with her hair all curled.

"How do I look?" she'd asked me.

I shrugged and didn't take my eyes off the TV. One of those bad reality shows about renovating houses was on. Mrs. McGraw watched them a whole lot, and even though I'd never tell anybody, I had started to kinda like them. I'd even come out of my room and sit on the couch to watch them with her when one of my favorites was on.

"What do I know?" I said. "I'm blind."

She swatted at my arm. "Ha-ha," she said. "All right. Well, you and Lila be good for Mrs. McGraw, please. She

96

just called to say she'll be over in about ten minutes. She's finishing something up at her house."

I snorted. The show I was watching would also be over in ten minutes. Which meant I was pretty dang sure what Mrs. McGraw was busy with at her house. When she got here, I'd have to ask her what she thought of the color they'd painted the bathroom. The grape-purple color seemed awful tacky to me, honestly.

I looked up at Beth. "Where are you going?" I asked. "On a date with *Vanessa*?"

I'd expected her to say "No!" or get annoyed with me for teasing. But instead, she just ruffled my hair and made her way to the front door. "You'll probably be asleep by the time I get home, so I'll see you in the morning."

I took that as a yes.

Anyway, I ain't sure when Vanessa will be coming over to check up on Lila, but I know there's a lot I still gotta do with her training. Like getting her better on the leash. We ain't done a ton of work on that yet. I make a mental note to watch some videos on leash training tonight and maybe then start working on that tomorrow. I wonder if it'll be tricky, holding her leash in one hand and the cane in the other and trying not to—

"Augh!"

The tip of the cane gets caught in a crack again, and before I can do anything about it I've run smack into the hard rubber grip, adding another bruise to the constellation forming on my belly.

Heat rushes into my cheeks, and my fists begin to clench. For a second, I ain't sure if I'm gonna cry or scream. All I know is, now I'm mad. The rage hits like a tornado touching down in the spring—all the conditions are right, but that still don't give you a whole lot of warning. I squeeze the grip of my cane before pulling my arm back and hurling it with all my strength down the sidewalk, away from me.

"Hadley!" Cilia yells at me, just as I hear the cane clatter to the concrete. I can't see where it landed, but I don't think it's real far away. Apparently all my strength ain't that much.

And just like a tornado, it's over as quick as it got here. There's still a storm—still a raging, rolling thunder in my chest. But the worst part, the spiraling whirlwind of frustration, has passed. I flop down, sitting on the curb, as Cilia's shoes thwack past me. I hear the *snap, snap* of the cane collapsing, folding up into its smaller size. Then she's sitting on the curb next to me. But I don't look at her.

"Listen," Cilia says. Her voice is quiet, but firm. "I know this is hard, but—"

"No, you don't," I interrupt, because I can't help myself. "You don't know anything. You ain't blind. Never have been. So what do you know about how hard this is?"

Cilia doesn't answer for a minute. Then she sighs. "That's . . . a fair point. Okay. I don't know exactly how hard it is to lose my vision the way you are. But I do know—and this is going to sound harsh, but I need you to hear me, Hadley—whether you want to acknowledge it or not, your vision is getting worse. As hard as it is right now, it's going to get harder. Especially if you aren't prepared. But this . . ." She slips the folded cane onto my lap. "This part does get easier. And it won't make everything easier, I know, but it will help as your sight gets worse. All this mobility stuff is going to be really important. And it's tough now, but it gets better. You just have to give it time."

"It just . . . It ain't fair," I tell her. I lean forward, resting my forehead against my knees so I ain't gotta look at anything as I whine. Because even I know that's exactly what I'm doing. Whining. I'm tired and irritated and, truth be told, ashamed. Both because of my outburst and because I'm struggling so much with something even little kids can do. "I didn't ask for none of this. For this stupid eye condition. Or to have to move to this stupid town because my stupid mama had to go and . . ."

I trail off. I hadn't meant to bring up Mama. It's the first time I've so much as mentioned her in weeks. And now there are hot, angry tears in my eyes. I don't look up.

I ain't sure how much Cilia knows about Mama, how much Beth would've told her when she got me these lessons. But my mobility teacher don't ask questions. Instead, she just rests a hand on my shoulder.

"I know," she says. "I know it's not fair. And no one can make it fair. But you've got people here who want to help. You just have to let us."

She stands up after a second, and I hear her dusting off her pants. I rub my wet eyes on my arm before looking up at her again.

"Come on, Hadley," she says. "I think our lesson is done for the day. We'll give this a try again next week. If that's all right with you."

I take a deep breath before getting to my feet. I snap the cane back together and touch the tip to the sidewalk, holding my hand in the correct posture again. Then I look up at Cilia, who's watching me. Waiting.

Slowly, I nod.

Then I start walking past her, back toward the community center, my cane sweeping in time with my steps.

Chapter Eleven

When I first told Joey and Maya that I was legally blind and that my vision was gonna get worse, they asked a lot of questions.

"How will you read?"

"How will you use a computer?"

"Does this mean you won't want to watch movies anymore? Because you can't see them?"

"Will you still be able to take pictures on your phone? Can you see the pictures we tag you in?"

"How many fingers am I holding up right now?"

That last one came from Joey, but before he could lift his arm up to hold fingers in front of my face, Maya grabbed his wrist and yanked it right back down.

"Pretty sure that's rude," she told him.

I'm not sure if it was rude or not, but it was annoying. Every time anybody—even grown-ups sometimes—finds out I'm blind, they put up their hand and ask how many fingers they're holding up. Like they're testing me. The answer is almost always three.

I didn't know how to answer the rest of their questions. I had no idea how reading or taking pictures or watching movies was gonna work yet. I could still do all that stuff—though it had definitely gotten a bit harder—but if the doctor was right and my vision was just gonna keep getting worse, I didn't know what that would mean.

"You know," Maya said, letting go of Joey's arm. "I'm legally blind without my glasses on."

"No, you ain't," I said. "The doctor says you're only legally blind if your vision is that way *with best correction*, which I think means glasses. So you can't be legally blind without glasses on, because the glasses fix it. You just got bad eyes without them on."

"Oh," she said. "Okay."

We were sitting on the school bus, heading home. We all lived on the same bus route, just a few miles apart. Which meant we got to spend a little extra time every morning and afternoon with each other. Normally I liked that, but today I was kinda ready to just go home to Mama.

I'd known for a while I was legally blind—since my last eye doctor visit when he said my vision had officially reached that point. My friends knew my vision was bad, but I hadn't told them it'd be getting worse. If Mama really wanted me to possibly take some kind of classes in the next year or two, though, I knew I'd have to be honest with my friends about what was going on. Besides, keeping it from them had been hard enough. We weren't the sorta friends who kept things from each other usually.

Still, I was wishing I had kept it to myself. Because all these questions just made me feel tired and worried.

And then Joey asked me one question I did know the answer to.

"Are you scared?" he asked. "About it getting even worse?"

"No."

It was the first time I'd ever outright lied to them before.

"That's good," Maya said. "I think I'd be scared. But I'm glad you're not. But if you ever need help with things—as you go blind or whatever—we'll be there. We can help."

"Yeah," Joey said. "We can definitely help with whatever you need."

"Thanks, y'all," I said. Though I knew that they couldn't.

When I got home, Mama was on the phone, having one of those conversations where she sounded real stressed out. This was in the winter, a few weeks before Christmas last year, and she'd stopped working for Dr. Parker months ago. Those calls, the ones I later learned were with lawyers, had only started in the last several weeks.

I made myself a bowl of cereal and sat down on the couch watching a rerun of some old sitcom about people living in New York City while I waited for Mama's call to wrap up. It took another half hour or so, and another episode of the show was playing when Mama finally hung up the phone, dropping it onto the kitchen counter with a huff, before coming to sit on the other end of the couch.

"Is everything okay?"

"It's fine, Bean. Don't worry about it."

I didn't know it then, but I wasn't the only one telling lies that day.

"How was school?"

"It was okay. But I told Joey and Maya what the doctors said, about me being really legally blind now."

"Oh?"

"Yeah." I put down my long-empty bowl of cereal. "They were . . . They weren't mean about it or anything. They were just . . . weird. They asked a lot of questions I don't got answers to. And then Joey asked me if I'm scared."

Mama was watching me. I could feel her eyes on my face, even though I had my head turned toward the TV, where two of the characters were about to get married while their friends scrambled around, getting things ready but also accidentally making them worse. I'd seen this episode before.

"What did you tell him?" she asked.

"I said I wasn't scared."

"Is that the truth?"

"No."

"Oh, Bean." Mama scooted across the couch toward me, then wrapped her arms around my shoulders, pulling me into a hug. "It's all right to be scared."

"No it ain't," I say, burying my face in her shoulder. Her hair smelled like the coconut shampoo she always used. "It's embarrassing. Especially because people already get all sad for me when they find out what's going on with my sight. If they know I'm scared, too, it'll be even worse."

Mama squeezed a little tighter. "I understand you not

wanting people to know it scares you. It's not anyone's business but yours. But you don't gotta be embarrassed about being scared. You know change is coming. And change is scary sometimes."

"I thought you said it'll be okay, though. That I'll be okay even if I can't see?"

"You will be," Mama said. "But that doesn't mean you're not allowed to be scared about how things will change. There are a lot of things as you grow up where you'll know a change is coming. And even if you know you'll probably come out the other side of it all right, not knowing how you'll get there is scary. All you can do is keep pushing forward, do your best, and have faith that, even if it takes a while, you'll get through it."

The way Mama's voice shook a bit when she spoke made me think she was speaking from experience. And now, months later, I realize she was probably dealing with her own fears then, about what was coming in her future. Except, unlike me, her situation was her own fault.

I'd had no idea what was coming, though. All I knew was that I trusted Mama more than anyone. That if she told me I'd be okay, I would, and if she said it was all right to be scared, then it was.

"Okay," I murmured. "Thanks, Mama."

"As for Joey and Maya," she said, "just give them some time. They care a lot about you, and maybe the way they showed it today wasn't great. But they'll get better. And if they don't, just tell them how you feel. They're good kids and good friends. I think they'll listen."

"Maybe."

She hugged me for a minute longer before her cell phone started to ring in the next room. Her arms fell slowly away from me as she stood up. I could sense the shift in her. That probably sounds weird, but I didn't have to see to feel the tension coming off Mama right then.

"I have to get that," she said, her voice tired and shaky.

Then she went to the kitchen to answer the phone, and I went back to watching the silly TV show. With no idea that my eyesight wasn't the only big change ahead of me that I ought to be worried about.

Chapter Twelve

"Rise and shine!" Beth calls out, pushing open my bedroom door with only a single knock of warning. "It's a beautiful Saturday, and it's well past time to get up."

"Ugh. Go away." I yank the covers over my and Lila's heads. She's taken a real liking to sleeping under the blankets with me. I thought it'd be too hot for her, since she's got fur and all, but apparently she don't mind too much. And right now, she wiggles closer to me, burying her face against my side, like she ain't ready to get up either.

"Come on, y'all." Beth sighs. "It's nearly noon. I've already spent a couple hours working in my garden. And I don't have any clients today, so the three of us are gonna spend some time together."

"Later."

"Nope."

The covers are peeled back, and it's me—not the dog in the bed—that snarls at my sister.

"Oh, give me a chance, Hadley. I've got a great idea for what we're going to do this afternoon. It'll be fun."

"Doubt it," I mumble, keeping my forearms pressed to my face.

"Lord. And Mama said *I* was a dramatic teenager."

At the mention of Mama, I feel my stomach drop, like a weight pulling me down deeper into the mattress. I roll onto my side, facing away from Beth. Behind her, on the little wooden desk, the stack of Mama's letters gets higher every week. All unopened. I wrap my arm around Lila, pressing my face into her short fur.

"Hadley . . ." Beth's voice is soft all of a sudden. I hate it. "You know . . . she really wants to hear from you. If you want to go see her, we could—"

"If I get out of bed, will you drop it?"

"Drop it?"

"Mama," I say, my voice a bit muffled as I speak against Lila's neck. "If I get up, will you stop talking about her?"

Beth lets out this long, exasperated sigh. The thing is, she *was* a dramatic teenager. I was real little, sure, but I remember. And I recall that sigh, in particular, driving Mama up the wall. I don't bring it up though. Because Beth says, "Fine. If you get up, I promise not to talk about Mama anymore. Today, at least."

"Deal."

I give Lila a quick squeeze followed by a little shake as I push myself up. "Come on. If I gotta suffer, so do you."

Lila whines.

"Hey now," Beth says. "No one is gonna do any suffering. I told you—I have a nice afternoon planned. You know, we've hardly spent any time together since you got here, and the time we have has all been in this house. So I figured we'd go on a bit of an adventure. And get in some leash training with Lila while we're at it."

At the sound of her name, Lila rolls over and looks at Beth. Then she looks back at me with an expression that, if you ask me, seems to say, *Do I have to?* I give her a solemn nod.

"So get dressed," Beth says. "I'll put some food in Lila's bowl and grab you a banana to eat before we go, but don't worry, we'll have a bigger meal while we're out." She claps her hands together, all perky and excited, before leaving the room. Though she don't shut the bedroom door behind her.

I climb off the bed with a groan and walk over to the

dresser to get my clothes. I can feel Lila watching me from the bed, so I say, "You might as well go eat. I don't think we're getting out of this."

She huffs out a breath, but after a second or so, I hear her feet hit the floor, and she plods out of the room toward the kitchen.

Twenty minutes later, I'm standing at the front door with Beth, who's got my cane in one hand and Lila's leash in the other. She hands them both to me, and I frown.

"You're gonna be with me, right? So I don't think I need this," I say, trying to hand the cane back to her.

Beth pushes it back toward me. "I will be with you, but you still need to practice."

"Ugh."

"You're gonna have to start working with Lila on leash training by yourself soon," she reminds me. "Might as well get the feel of walking her while using a cane now."

"Whatever."

"I appreciate your enthusiasm, Baby Sister," she says. She looks down at Lila, who has flopped onto her side and closed her eyes, as if faking sleep. "And yours, Lila. Come on. Both y'all. Let's get moving." She picks up a backpack by the door and slings it over her shoulders.

I scowl at her calling me Baby Sister before kneeling down and hooking the leash onto Lila's collar, giving it a gentle tug to urge her back to her feet. She stands, but it's clear she ain't real happy about it. Can't say I blame her. The three of us have never gone anywhere together before. Not since bringing Lila home from the rescue. Really, the only person I've been out of the house with much is Mrs. McGraw, who takes me to see Cilia for my lessons.

This is gonna be weird. I just know it.

As soon as we reach the sidewalk, Beth switches into dog-trainer mode. She keeps a close eye on Lila and tells me how to correct her: how to keep her from pulling too hard or walking behind, how to get her to heel. All that stuff. She's brought a bag of baby carrots along to help, and to my surprise, Lila actually seems to be picking up on things pretty quickly. It probably shouldn't shock me, though, considering how fast she learned the other things I taught her, even if she wouldn't do them in front of anyone for a while. Today, I'm the one having the harder time. Turns out, holding a cane in one hand and a dog leash in the other is kinda tricky. Especially when I am still poking myself in the belly with my cane at least once every block or two.

"How'd you end up as a dog trainer, anyway?" I ask Beth

as we walk past the dog park. Lila's head turns to watch through the fence as some of the other dogs bark and chase each other around, but she keeps walking like she's supposed to, no growling or whining or trying to run off this time. "Good girl," I murmur, before looking over to Beth again. "I didn't even know you liked dogs."

"Just because we didn't have one growing up doesn't mean I didn't like them," she says. "I would've loved to have one as a kid, but Daddy was allergic, so . . ." She trails off for a minute, then clears her throat. "Anyway. Um, well, when I was nineteen or so, I volunteered at a dog rescue—not the one Vanessa runs. This was in another town, before I moved here. My roommate at the time was volunteering, so I decided I would, too. And I really enjoyed it. I found out I was pretty good with dogs, and I thought why not make it my job? So I found a dog obedience school in the area and convinced one of the trainers there to do an apprenticeship with me."

"How'd you end up at Right Choice Rescue?"

When she answers, Beth's voice is brighter, happier than she's been since I came here. I realize she's excited I asked, which almost makes me wish I hadn't. But the truth is, I've been wondering this for a while. If I'd had to imagine a future for the big sister who left Mama and me all those years ago, this wouldn't have been it. Though, I guess I didn't really have an alternative in mind, either.

Honestly, I just don't feel like I know Beth at all. And I'm torn between wanting to keep it that way and wanting to figure out what has happened to the girl who taught me how to do cartwheels in the backyard or who ran up and down the hallways with me on her shoulders until Mama hollered at us to stop before one of us got hurt.

"Well, when I moved here, I decided to try and start a business. So people could hire me to come and train their dogs or do some obedience work if they were having trouble. I put a bunch of flyers up and made a website and all that. And after a few months, Vanessa gave me a call. She'd just opened the rescue and had a couple dogs she thought she could find a good home for if they just had a bit more training. So I took the job, got those dogs on their best behavior, and a month later, they were both adopted. So she asked me to stick around. I still work with family dogs, too. In fact, that's most of my work. But I think my time with Right Choice is probably what I find most rewarding."

I nod.

"You know, Vanessa is always looking for volunteers, if you ever wanna come to work with me sometime. I know you're busy with Lila, but you could visit the rescue like once a week or so, help out for a few hours. I could show you what I do every day. And the dogs always love more company."

"I don't think so."

Beth's excited expression falters, erased by disappointment. I turn my eyes down to Lila so I don't gotta look at her.

We only walk for about twenty minutes or so before Beth leads us off the sidewalk and onto a dirt path that snakes its way up a small hill. "There's not a lot going on in this town," she tells me, a bit of that cheer returning to her voice, "but we do have this very cute little park here, with a perfect picnic spot. Watch your step, by the way. The ground's not real even. And don't let Lila sniff like that— she'll trip you up. Give her leash a light tug just to get her attention—there you go. And we're almost there now."

I try not to get too frustrated with Beth telling me what to do. But it doesn't go as bad as the night she tried to help me teach Lila to "Come." Today Lila seems to be actually listening, and Beth's advice is helpful. Not as overwhelming as before.

We make it to the top of the hill, where there are several picnic tables scattered around. It seems like most of them are already taken—being a Saturday afternoon in July and all—but Beth leads us over to an open one and helps me tether Lila's leash to one of the table legs before taking off her backpack.

"I figured we could have our lunch here today," she says, unzipping the backpack. She pulls out some sandwich bags, two bottles of water, and a few packs of potato chips. "It just seemed like a real waste of a nice day to stay inside. We could all use some fresh air."

I know "we all" actually means "you"—because from what she's said, Beth spends a lot of her day outside working with dogs. It's me that only goes outside when Lila's gotta go pee or during my weekly mobility lesson. But I don't bother pointing it out. Instead, I just open the sandwich bag she gives me and sniff inside.

"Peanut butter and jelly?"

"Yep. I remember it was your favorite thing to have for lunch when you were little. I hope you still like it?"

I just shrug. But truth is, I do. When I see she's cut it diagonally, though, the way Mama always did, a pang of sadness hits me real hard. I force myself to take a big bite and look away so Beth can't see my face.

I don't *want* to miss Mama. I'm still furious with her. I ain't opened any of her letters or answered any of her calls from jail. I won't ever forgive her for being a liar. But sometimes, these little things, like this stupid sandwich, will make me think of her. Of the way she'd always pack my lunch for school with a note that said *I love you, Bean!* With a smiley face at the end. I always rolled my eyes at that, but now that I don't have it, it feels wrong. Or how she knew just the right way to braid my hair so it wouldn't come loose halfway through the day. Or how we'd spend almost every night on the couch together, one blanket wrapped around the both of us, while she'd read me books. We'd been halfway through *Tuck Everlasting* when she got sentenced. I still don't know how it ends.

"Oh, Lila, don't snap at bees! You're gonna get stung in the mouth!"

I'm glad for Beth's voice pulling me out of my thoughts, because I was starting to get choked up. And crying in public—or in front of her—is the last thing I want.

I look down at Lila. I can't see the bumblebee flying around, but I can hear it and kinda guess where it might be based on the direction her big, square jaws keep snapping in. I reach out my leg and nudge her with my foot. She looks at me.

"Leave the bee alone."

She huffs and puts her head down on her paws.

"I think Lila is more dramatic than me," I tell Beth. "She makes that huffing sound an awful lot."

"I'd say it's a toss up." Beth takes a bite of her sandwich, then says, "She's doing so much better, though. Before you got here, I never could have imagined being able to take her for an outing like this. Half the time I'd put the leash on her, and she'd just lie down and refuse to get up. She's come a long way. All thanks to you."

"She's all right. For a dog," I admit. "I still ain't a dog person."

Beth chuckles. "Sure. Whatever you say, Hadley. Now, if I remember right, you had a stuffed dog as a kid that you dragged around everywhere."

"No! Pickles was a fox, not a dog. Big difference."

"Right. My mistake." She shakes her head. "Lord. That thing got so disgusting. Then when Mama tried to wash it, it was ruined. You were so upset. I don't think I ever saw anyone cry so much."

"Is that when you gave me Bunny Bear?"

"My stuffed pig? Yeah. I felt bad that you'd lost your favorite stuffed animal, so I figured you could have my old one. I was too big for it by then anyway."

"Why did you name a stuffed pig Bunny Bear?"

"Because I was four when Daddy got it for me. And I guess I wasn't good at knowing what different animals looked like. I don't know. But it stuck."

"I did like Bunny Bear," I admit. "But I remember staying up all night with my eyes half open trying to watch it because you told me that when I was asleep, it got up and walked around the room and played with my other toys."

Beth grins. "Oh, I forgot I did that. Well, I might have been being nice giving it to you, but you were still my little sister. I had to mess with you somehow. Mama was so mad when she found out, though. Every morning for like a week you looked like a tiny zombie because you were so tired. Whatever happened to Bunny Bear anyway?"

"I . . . dunno. Don't remember."

That's a lie. I remember exactly what happened to that stuffed pig. I was so upset after Beth left that, when she hadn't come home after a week, I tossed Bunny Bear into the trash. Mama tried to talk me out of it, but I didn't wanna look at it anymore.

There's a bit of a pause, then Beth says, "I've missed you, you know. I know I didn't see you after I left home, but that didn't mean I stopped thinking about you."

I look down at Lila again, watch her lick her paw so I ain't gotta look at my sister.

"I'm sorry," she says, voice quiet. "That I wasn't there. But I'm glad I get to spend time with you now. I know you might not feel the same—and I wish it were under different circumstances—but . . . but I'm happy to get to be in your life again."

I open my mouth to ask the question I've been wanting to ask for weeks, but I close it again. Real tight. Because I don't want her to know it's the thing I've been thinking all this time. After a minute, though, the urge is too strong to avoid, and I blurt out, "Why'd you leave? Why did you leave Mama and me?"

"I . . . It's . . ." Beth lets out a sigh. "It's a long story. And old news. No sense digging it back up now."

I scoff. "Fine. Whatever."

"Hadley . . . I am sorry."

But she's not sorry enough to tell me why she left us, apparently. So I ain't sure what that's worth. Or why I bothered bringing it up. All it's done is remind me how much it hurt all those years ago, when she left. I feel the weight of that settle on me. I wish I was back in my room, under my covers, alone with just Lila.

I finish off my sandwich and bag of chips in silence. Beth gets done eating right around the same time.

"If you're ready, we can head out of here. There's some other places I wanted to show you around town. There's this cute bookshop a few blocks from here. I thought maybe we could pick out a book to read together?"

"Together?"

"Sure," she says. "I thought if we found one, I could read it out loud to you? Mama used to read out loud to me all the time as a kid. Even when I was in high school, sometimes after she put you to bed and Daddy was working late, she'd turn off the TV and grab a book and read it to me. I thought maybe you and I could do that?"

I stare at her for a minute, surprised. I had no idea Mama had done that with Beth, too. Most of my memories of the two of them weren't too nice. When they'd bicker or yell at each other. I didn't know they'd ever gotten along well enough to do something like that.

Beth gathers up the garbage on the picnic table. "I'll be right back. There's a trash can right over there. Then we can walk to the bookshop."

Once she's walked off, I stand up and unfold my cane. Then I bend down and untether Lila from the table, looping her leash back around my hand. When I straighten back up, I notice something I hadn't before.

There's a girl at one of the other picnic tables. One of the ones that's close by. She's got wavy, dark brown pigtails and looks to be about my age maybe. And she's staring right back at me. Just *staring*.

I look down, wondering if I have jelly on my shirt or something. And then notice the cane in my hand.

I think that must be what she's staring at. But I can't see her expression real well. I can't tell if she's looking at me because she thinks I'm weird. Or because she feels sorry for me. But I don't like it, either way. It makes my skin itch. I feel embarrassed and exposed.

I'm overcome with the sudden desire to throw my cane at her. Or just to throw it away altogether. I don't care how helpful it might be. I don't want people staring at me. And I know this girl can't be the first. She's only the first I've noticed. I bet people stare at me all the time and I just can't see them. The thought leaves me feeling sick.

I glare at her, then turn away real fast, just as Beth walks back to the table. "Okay. Ready to do some more training with Lila on the way to the bookstore?"

"I'm going home," I mutter, shoving past Beth and

pulling Lila along behind me as I head for the path that led us up this hill.

It takes Beth a second to start following us—she's still gotta get her backpack—and by the time she catches up, we're already halfway down the hill.

"Hadley?" she asks. "Hadley, slow down, you're gonna trip."

"I'm fine!" I snap. "Just because I'm blind now don't mean you gotta tell me what to do. Don't treat me different just because I can't see!"

"I wasn't." And now Beth sounds irritated, too. "I'd tell you to slow down either way. And what brought this on? I thought we were going to the bookstore? Why are you storming off like this?"

"I don't wanna go to your stupid bookstore."

"Hadley." As we hit the sidewalk, our feet back on flat pavement again, Beth manages to swerve in front of Lila and me, blocking our way. "What's the matter?"

"Nothing!"

Beth throws her hands in the air. "You know what? Fine. I don't know why I even bothered trying to have a nice day with you."

I freeze for a second, startled. It's the first time since I got here that Beth's actually raised her voice at me. She's sounded irritated or annoyed with me, sure, but never angry. She's angry now, though, and it's come on so sudden that I can't help but be shocked.

"I've tried and tried and *tried* to be patient with you," my sister says. "Because I know what you're going through ain't easy. I've tried to let it go when you've been rude because you're having a hard time right now. But, dang it, Hadley, I'm getting sick of it!"

"I didn't ask you to baby me because you feel sorry for me."

"I wasn't! I was just trying to be a good sister! And today—I wanted *one* nice day together—I tried to make everything relaxed and fun. But I guess that wasn't good enough! Because without warning you storm off and snap at me and won't tell me what's going on."

"And I didn't ask for a nice day!" I yell back at her. "I didn't ask you to do any of this! This sucks. All of it. Being blind and Mama being gone and having to live with you! I didn't want any of it!"

"Do you think you're the only one who's having a hard time with all this? Do you think I planned to be a twenty-four-year-old taking care of my little sister? You're not the only one put in a situation they didn't ask for, Hadley!"

Woof! Woof! Woof!

Beth and I both stop yelling and look down. Lila is standing right between us, her massive, boxy head turning from one side to the other, glaring at each of us in turn as she barks. I think Beth and I are both startled—Lila grumbles and huffs and groans an awful lot, but she don't bark much at all. Yet, here she is, scolding my sister and me for yelling at each other.

Even after she stops barking, she keeps glaring at us. Like she's daring us to do it again. A few people walk by us, and even though I can't hear what they're saying, I'm pretty sure they're talking about Beth and me. We were just yelling at each other in public, after all. But I'm too angry and upset to be embarrassed.

I look back up at my sister. "So is that how you really feel, then?" I ask. My voice is quiet now. Not quite a whisper, but close. "Were you lying earlier? About being happy to have me back in your life?"

"No," Beth says. Her voice is softer now, too, and the way it cracks is painfully familiar. She sounds so much like Mama whenever Mama was on the verge of crying. "I love you, Hadley. What I just said . . . I'm sorry. I—"

"It don't matter," I say, and I move to walk past her again. "Let's just go."

"Hadley . . ."

But I'm already walking down the sidewalk. Lila's moving along next to me, at a perfect heel, and I can feel the twitch in her leash every time she turns her head to look up at me, like she's checking that I'm okay. I pretend not to notice. I don't want anyone, not even Lila, feeling sorry for me.

A minute later, Beth falls into step beside me. Neither of us say a word to each other the rest of the walk back to her house.

Chapter Thirteen

On top of sending letters every week, Mama keeps calling. Every. Single. Night.

After she first picked me up six weeks ago, Beth had to call a special number on her cell phone and set it up so Mama could make calls to her from the jail. I told her she was wasting her time. That I wasn't gonna talk to her. But Beth did it anyway, and now every evening, right at dinnertime, her phone rings.

"Hi, Mama," Beth says after waiting through the automated voice at the start of the call. "Yeah, it's me . . . I'm doing all right. How are you?"

It's weird hearing Beth talk to her, even after all these weeks. At first, it had seemed like she didn't know what to say and was just filling the silence until she could get off the phone. Now, though, Beth seems more comfortable. She always spends the first few minutes of every call telling Mama about her job or Vanessa or plans she's made with her friends. I don't know if that means they get along now or what. And I don't know how I feel about it, either.

I don't gotta think about it for long, though, because after a few minutes, Beth pauses and says the same thing she does every single night:

"Yep. Hadley's right here. Let me ask her."

Then she turns to me. The first few times, she asked if I wanted to talk to Mama. But after I said no enough times, loud enough I knew Mama could hear it on the other end, she stopped asking. At least with words. Now she just looks at me and waits.

Tonight, though, when Beth turns to look at me, I'm already leaving the room. As soon as the phone started ringing, I went to rinse off my plate in the sink. Beth usually makes me do the dishes on nights when she cooks, but I can do them later. For now, I'm going to my room, and Lila is following close behind.

I hear Beth sigh as she says, "Um, she's busy right now, Mama. She's . . . she's doing some training with Lila . . . Yeah, that's going pretty well. She's real good with the dog, already made some good progress with her . . . Uh-huh, she's still doing that mobility training. She's getting lots of practice with her new cane."

I grit my teeth and shut the bedroom door behind Lila and me so I ain't gotta hear Beth talk about me anymore.

I guess there's a limit on how long they let you talk on the phone when you're in jail, because Mama's calls only last about fifteen minutes. But tonight, when Beth gets off the phone, she comes to my bedroom door. And for once, she knocks and waits to come in.

"Hadley," she says from the hallway. "Can I come in a minute?"

"I guess."

I'm sitting on my bed, holding one end of a short rope toy as Lila, standing in front of me, tugs on the other. Lila hadn't really shown any interest in toys until Beth brought this one home a few days ago. The minute Lila saw the rope, she got more excited than I'd ever seen her. And now, pretty much any time I sit down, she grabs it and runs over, hoping to coax me into a game. She braces her front legs and clenches her jaw as she pulls, sometimes even letting out a little play growl. Lila's pretty strong, so when she inevitably manages to pull the rope out of my hand, she always freezes, waiting for me to take it again so we can pick up right where we left off.

The door opens, and Beth watches us play for a minute. I think I even hear her chuckle a little before she moves into the room, sitting down in the desk chair across from my bed.

"Can I talk to you?" she asks.

"Ain't that what you're doing right now?" I ask, still watching Lila as we continue our game.

Beth and I ain't talked much since our argument by the park a couple days ago. I didn't think either of us had anything left to say, but apparently she does now.

"Hadley . . ."

I sigh and let go of the rope. Lila tries to offer it to me again, but I shake my head. "Go on," I tell the dog. "We'll play later."

Dramatic as always, Lila huffs, then just lets the rope drop from her mouth and onto the floor. Clearly disappointed in me.

"Blame Beth," I say. "She's the one who wants to talk."

Lila looks over at my sister before hopping up onto the bed beside me, head turned to glare at Beth. Like she's also waiting to hear what's so important as to stop her playtime.

"So . . ." Beth says, "I was just talking to Mama . . ."

"Yeah. So?"

"She misses you, Hadley. A lot."

I shrug.

"You know . . . she can have visitors. They have visitation days. She'd really love to see you."

I don't say nothing.

"I know it's a long drive back down to Tennessee," Beth continues, "but I'd be happy to do it. It'd be good for all of us. We could even make a day of it. Like a little road trip. We could stop by one of those big shopping malls along the way. Or maybe meet up with some of your friends in Tennessee and get dinner after? You can tell Mama all about your training with Cilia and what you've been up to with Lila and—"

"No."

"But, Hadley—"

"No!" I say, louder this time. Loud enough it makes Lila jump. "I don't want to see her. Ever again."

"Don't say that."

"Why shouldn't I?" I demand. "Mama taught me never to steal or lie. She taught me that those were bad things. And then she did both. Why should I want anything to do with her?"

"Because she still loves you," Beth says. "She made a

mistake. A real bad one. But she did it because she wanted to take care of you. I'm not saying that's an excuse or that it was right. But it doesn't change how much she cares about you, Hadley."

"I don't care." I fold my arms over my chest. "I don't want nothing to do with her. Besides, I thought you were about done trying to have nice days with me after what happened on Saturday."

Beth looks down at her feet. "I shouldn't have said the things I did that day. I'm sorry."

"Don't be," I say. "You weren't wrong. Neither of us asked for any of this. No sense lying about that and pretending we're happy."

"But we can make the best of it," she offers. "Hadley, I did mean what I said that morning—I'm happy to have you back in my life, even if I didn't . . . didn't plan for it to be this way. I *want* to do nice things for you and spend time with you. It's just . . . it's hard when it feels like I can't do anything without getting you mad at me."

I shrug. I don't know how to tell her that it ain't her fault I got upset on Saturday—that it was really because I saw that girl staring at me. And I don't know that I wanna tell her that, either. Because I know she don't always deserve the way I treat her, and sometimes, I do feel bad about it. But I don't know how to stop it. I got no clue how to stop being angry or how to not take it out on her. So maybe if she just accepts it now—that it ain't gonna change—then she'll stop trying so hard.

"Anyway . . . I don't see why you're the one telling me I should, considering you don't even like Mama."

"That's not true," Beth says.

"Ain't it, though?" I ask. "You took off and then never called or wrote or nothing. Not to me or her. If you can go off and decide never to see her again, why can't I?"

Beth don't answer, and for a long moment, I don't think she's going to. I mean, what else is there to say? She just sits there, looking down at her bare feet on the carpet. But finally, she takes a deep breath and looks up at me again.

"What I did—leaving like that—it's exactly why I think you should see her, Hadley."

"I don't want—"

"Just hear me out a second," she says. "I won't make you do anything you really don't want to. But . . . But you asked me the other day why I left, and I didn't tell you. Truth is, I'm real embarrassed about the whole thing. I ain't proud of it. And if I could do it over again, I would." She swallows, loud enough I can hear it. "After . . . After Daddy died, Mama and I didn't get along well. We were both sad and angry, and we took it out on each other. We both said some not-so-kind things to each other, but I said the worst."

I watch my sister, my narrow field of vision focusing on her face as best as I can. But she ain't meeting my eyes.

"I'd already been planning to leave," Beth explains. "I'd graduated. I'd saved up money to get an apartment with some friends. But the night before I was supposed to move out, Mama and I got into a fight. And I . . . at the end of it, I told her . . . I said . . ." Beth's voice gets real shaky, and I think she might be about to cry. "I told her that I wished it had been her. Instead of Daddy, I mean. That I wished . . . I wished she was the one who'd died."

"Oh." The sound leaves my mouth on an exhale, but I hadn't meant to make a noise at all.

I don't remember that argument. I was pretty little when Beth left, after all. But I do remember her and Mama yelling a lot. And when I asked why, both of them would always just tell me not to worry about it. The morning after Beth went away, I found Mama sitting on the couch in the living room crying. All these years, I'd assumed it was because Beth had moved out. But now I see there was more to it than that.

Still, this throws me for a loop. The older sister I grew up with, the one I remember, was bubbly and energetic and maybe a little dramatic, but . . . Even now, as upset as I've been with her, I can't imagine her saying something that mean. Just thinking something like that is terrible. And not the kinda thing I'd have expected from Beth.

"I didn't mean it," Beth says quickly. "I felt awful about it the minute the words left my mouth. But instead of saying I was sorry, I . . . I left. And I was too ashamed to talk to her again after that. Mama called me, and I didn't answer. And she kept calling, but I . . . couldn't talk to her. After a while, she called less and less. She stopped after a year or so. By then, I didn't just feel ashamed for what I had said but for taking so long to apologize. So I . . . I stayed away. And I've regretted it. A lot."

"That's a stupid reason to stop talking to us," I snap. I'm angry at her. It's an old, heavy anger that sits on my chest. It mingles with something even more raw: grief. The grief and mourning I felt and pushed away years ago, when I first realized Beth wasn't coming back. It's all stirred up inside me again now.

I'm not upset with her for what she said to Mama, but that she didn't just apologize and come home when she could have. I'm angry at her for letting that argument take her away from me. When I hadn't done nothing wrong.

"You're right," she says. "It was. Especially because I know Mama would have forgiven me. I made a mistake, I did a bad thing, but she would have forgiven me. I just never gave her the chance."

"And what about me?" I ask. "Were you too busy thinking about Mama to consider me? I thought you'd come home. I waited and waited. I knew y'all argued, but *I* never fought with you. I thought you'd come back for . . . for me. And I've been so, so mad at you that you didn't. And I . . ."

I trail off. I wish I hadn't said any of that, because now there are tears springing to my eyes. And I hate myself for being this pathetic.

"I'm sorry, Baby Sister."

"Hadley," I correct.

"Hadley. I'm . . . I'm sorry. I was young, and stupid, and you were . . . you were caught in the middle. I never meant for that to happen. I wish I could change things."

I look away. Not because I'm mad at her, but because I ain't sure what else I'm supposed to say to all this.

Beth don't make me dwell on it too long, though.

"I'm not gonna make you do anything you don't want to,

Hadley," she says again. "But take it from me—seeking forgiveness ain't easy. Especially from the people you hurt. But Mama's trying. She's trying real hard. You don't gotta forgive her. That's up to you. But . . . at least know what you're doing, okay? I don't want you to have the same kinda regrets I do."

"What about you?" I ask. "You've been talking to her again. Did you apologize? Did she forgive you?"

"I did apologize," Beth says. "And . . . she has. She forgave me right away. It don't make what I did right or better. It doesn't mean it goes away. But we're trying. Both of us. It's hard and uncomfortable, but . . . it's better than losing her forever, you know?"

When I don't say nothing in response, Beth gets to her feet. I keep my head turned and listen as she quietly walks out of the room and shuts the door behind her.

After she's gone, I move to look at Lila, who's still lying on the bed beside me. She's staring at me with her big, dark eyes. She pushes herself into a sitting position so she can lick my cheek.

The best thing about Lila is, she don't expect me to say nothing. I lean against her, wrapping one arm around her boxy frame, glad for the company that won't judge the confused, frustrated tears sliding down my cheeks.

Chapter Fourteen

Mama never told me she was worried about money, but looking back, I probably should've picked up on it sooner.

I should've noticed the way she'd let out a frustrated sigh every time she opened our empty fridge. Or the strain in her voice when she promised me she'd come up with the money I needed to go on a class trip. Or the way she'd bury her face in her hands while sitting at the kitchen table, with a pile of bills in front of her.

The first time I really started to think that maybe something might be wrong was about a year ago, when Mama was still working for Dr. Parker.

I'd walked into the kitchen, feeling a bit frustrated as I tried to button a pair of jeans that just wouldn't fit. Mama was at the table, that pile of bills in front of her. She wasn't looking at them, though. Instead, she seemed to be staring at the wall. I didn't think much of it, because I had my own things to be worried about.

"Mama," I said with a groan as I walked over to the table. "Mama, I think I need new clothes."

It took her a minute to respond. But after a second, she turned to look at me. "What was that, Hadley Bean? Sorry. I was just . . . What's wrong?"

"My clothes," I said. "I think I need some new ones. Especially jeans."

"What's wrong with the clothes you have now?"

"Look." I gestured to the pants I was struggling to button. The jeans showed way more ankle than they had when we'd bought them at the start of the school year. And they were way too tight around my hips now, too. I could barely pull them on, let alone get them fastened. "I just got these out of my closet thinking I could wear them tomorrow, but they don't fit. Almost none of my pants do anymore."

"Oh, don't be dramatic," she said, pushing herself to her feet. "I'm sure most of them still fit. Come on. Let's go take a look."

But Mama was wrong. Of all the clothes she'd bought me at the start of the school year, only one pair of jeans still

142

looked all right, and I'd been wearing and washing them constantly, so the knees were starting to wear out.

Mama looked down at the pile of too-small clothes on my bed in disbelief. "How did you outgrow all these so fast?"

I shrug. "I dunno. But I can't wear this stuff anymore. Most of the pants won't even pull all the way up now."

"Puberty." Mama sighed. "I can't believe you're growing up this fast. We'll figure something out. For now, you have leggings that fit, right?"

"Yeah," I said. "But I can't wear them to school."

"How come?"

"It's against dress code unless you're wearing them with a dress that's down to your knees," I told her. "It's stupid."

Mama nodded. "Yeah, that is stupid."

"So," I said, sitting down on my bed next to the pile of jeans. "Can we go shopping this weekend or something?"

"I don't know if we can do it this weekend," Mama said, turning to start walking out of the room and back toward the kitchen. "But we'll definitely do it soon."

"Can it please be this weekend?" I asked, hurrying after her. "Mama, the end-of-year dance is next week. And then fifth grade graduation on Friday. I need jeans that look all right for those. I can't wear the ones with holes in them."

"I forgot all about the dance," Mama admitted as she poured herself a glass of sweet tea. "Shoot. Can't you wear one of your dresses?"

"Most of my dresses are too short for dress code now. Or are too tight. The only dress that fits is this year's Easter dress," I explained. "Way too fancy for a school dance. Besides, almost none of the girls will be wearing dresses to the dance or to graduation. If I did, I'd be teased for being too dressed up. Almost everyone wears jeans and a nice shirt. Please, Mama, we gotta get me some new clothes."

Mama took a long drink of her tea before putting the glass back down on the counter and turning away from me. "I'll . . . I'll figure something out."

"So we're gonna go clothes shopping this weekend?"

She didn't answer me. Just kept her back to me, facing the window over the sink.

"Mama?"

"Yeah." She turned on the faucet, rinsed out her cup, and turned around slowly. "Yeah. I'll take care of it, Hadley Bean. Don't worry about it. I'll make sure everything works out."

"Mama, is everything okay?"

"Of course it is." She walked over to me and wrapped her arms around me, squeezing me into a hug. "The only thing that's not okay is how fast you're growing! How am I supposed to keep you in clothes if you won't stop getting taller." She ruffled my hair, messing up my hair as I tried to shrug out of her reach. She laughed. But it still sounded a little strained. "You're gonna be as tall as me soon."

"I'm gonna be taller than you eventually."

"We'll see about that."

I reached up to smooth out my hair again. "So . . . everything's all right?"

"Don't worry about a thing, Bean." She leaned forward and gave me a kiss on the forehead. "Everything will work out. I'll take care of us, I promise."

And that was the thing—I never really thought about our money troubles because Mama always told me not to. She always said we'd be fine, that she'd take care of things. And she always did. She always came through with whatever I needed.

Of course, I had no idea that one way she'd been "taking care of us" was by stealing from Dr. Parker.

Chapter Fifteen

Beth wants me to start taking Lila to the dog park near her house. She says it's just as important for Lila to learn how to socialize with other dogs as it is with other people. But considering she also tells me how many kids in the neighborhood take their dogs there, I'm guessing Lila ain't the only one she thinks ought to be socializing.

I know if I don't do it, she'll just keep bugging me about it. So one afternoon, after watching one of those house remodeling shows with Mrs. McGraw, I get Lila leashed up.

Apparently Beth had a talk with Mrs. McGraw about me going places by myself in the neighborhood, because she doesn't try to argue as much anymore about whether or not it's safe. That ain't to say she makes it easy, though.

"Don't go anywhere but the dog park, you hear?"

"Yes, ma'am."

"And call me if you're gonna be more than an hour or two. You got that cell phone of yours, right?"

"Yes, ma'am."

"If I call you and you don't answer, I'm coming out looking for you."

"Okay."

"Your sister says you're fine and I ought to let you go out and practice with your cane. But if you get lost or hurt or something—"

"I'll be *fine*. Can I go?"

"Don't give me that attitude, young lady. No need to be rude."

"Can I go, *please*?"

Despite herself, Mrs. McGraw gives a snort of laughter at that. And I might smile back at her. Just a little.

"All right. Go on then. Don't forget your cane."

I groan, but I do grab my cane as I head out the door and down the sidewalk with Lila.

I almost hate to admit it, but walking with Lila like this is a little easier now than it was a few weeks ago. My cane still jabs into my stomach sometimes, but I also don't gotta look at my feet no more. Instead, I can focus on correcting

Lila on the leash, keeping her at a good heel the way Beth showed me. And Lila's doing pretty good at it, too.

"You know, Lila," I say when we're standing across the street from the dog park, listening for traffic like Cilia's been teaching me, "for a dog who was supposedly so hard to train, you actually learn things real quick. Makes me think you're just stubborn and know more than you let on."

I feel Lila's tail hit the back of my legs. Two quick wags. That's about all I ever expect from her.

I wait maybe longer than I need to before I cross the street. I don't hear any cars, and Beth says this part of town ain't real busy during the day. But I'm still feeling kinda nervous as I listen, and I keep second-guessing myself. It's silly. I used to cross streets by myself all the time. I ain't a little kid. But now that Cilia's been showing me safer ways to do it during mobility lessons—listening for the traffic that's moving in the same direction as me or the all-quiet and such—I'm actually trying to do what she says. I ain't used to relying on my ears yet.

After a minute, I decide there really ain't any cars coming, and I tug Lila with me as I walk across the street, toward the dog park, at top speed.

There ain't a lot of people here today, which I can't say

bothers me much. I keep Lila's leash on until we find an empty bench on the shady end of the park, under a few trees. Once I've gotten comfortable, I unhook Lila's leash and say, "Okay. Go on. Go play."

She don't move.

"You don't have to play with any of the other dogs," I tell her. "But at least go run around or something."

Lila looks up at me, then turns around and sits down with her back to the bench.

I sigh. "Fine. We'll just stay a few minutes. That way it'll at least get Beth off our backs."

The words have hardly left my mouth when I hear a scrambling noise and see a big black figure hurtling across the dog park and right at me. I don't even have time to stand up or move before two paws slam into my chest and a long, wet tongue begins lapping at my cheeks.

"Augh!"

"No, Pilot! Off!"

I shove at the chest of the large, fluffy dog while, from the other side, someone else pulls it back. Once it's off me, I stand up real quick and start wiping the dog drool off my face.

"Sorry. I'm real sorry," says the girl who's now holding

the dog by its collar. She looks to be about my age, with a round face and wavy brown pigtails. And I think she looks kinda familiar. "Pilot's big, but he's still a puppy. Only ten months old. And he just really likes people. I'm sorry. Are you all right?"

"Yeah, I'm fine."

I stare at her for a minute, trying to figure out where I know this girl from. And then it hits me, a flash of memory from a few days earlier.

I *have* seen her before. This girl was the one sitting at a picnic table, staring at me and my cane.

I tense up a bit, already feeling irritated, when the girl suddenly recognizes me, too.

"Oh!" she says. "I keep seeing you around! You and your dog were up on the hill the other day, right? At the picnic tables? I saw y'all there."

"Yeah," I mutter. I start looking around for Lila, who ain't sitting in front of the bench no more. I figure she probably ran off when the black dog jumped on me. I wanna find her quick, though, because I sure don't wanna stick around to listen to this girl tease me about my cane.

"I saw you a few weeks ago, too," she says. "When Pilot and I were leaving this dog park, actually. You were across the street. I tried to say hi, but I think you were heading somewhere."

It takes me a minute of looking around, my eyes straining for a glimpse of Lila, before I spot her. She ain't gone real far. She's behind the bench and is just sitting there, watching me and this girl and her dog through the wooden slats. I'm about to grab her leash and go over to her when I realize what the girl has just said.

"Huh?" I say, turning to face her. Then I remember. It was the first day I'd taken Lila for a walk. The day I'd tripped and Lila had run away from me, because we'd both been trying to avoid the too-friendly girl coming toward us. That was *this* girl. My face gets hot, embarrassed, wondering if she saw me fall that day.

If she did, she doesn't bring it up now.

"Yeah. I was hoping to say hi, but you took off so fast that day. And then again at the picnic tables. I'm glad I finally get to meet you now. I'm Shelby."

I just stare at her at first, not sure if I ought to be relieved she hasn't teased me about my cane or if I should still be wary. Also, I just . . . ain't real sure what to say to her. I haven't spent much time with anyone my age since I left Mama's house. It's pretty much just been Lila and Beth and

Mrs. McGraw. But Shelby is looking at me, still smiling but like she's expecting something, and after a too-long pause I manage to say:

"Uh . . . I'm Hadley."

"Nice to meet you, Hadley," she says. Then, with an embarrassed smile, she admits, "If I'm being honest, though, it's your dog I was really hoping to meet. No offense to you—I'm sure you're great, too, and I'd love to get to know you. But . . . I really love dogs, so whenever there's a new one in the neighborhood, I get a little excited. Kinda the way Pilot does with people."

"Oh."

"I almost came over and asked if I could pet her at the picnic tables," Shelby explains. "But then you left. So . . . can I say hi to her now? What's her name? Is she friendly?"

It takes a second for her words to set in, but then it all clicks. She's not making comments about my cane because that wasn't why she'd been staring at me to begin with. She was just interested in Lila. Maybe I ought to be a little hurt that this girl is more interested in getting to know a dog than me, but I prefer that to what I'd been imagining—that she thought I was weird or was gonna make fun of me for being blind. But Shelby don't say a word about any of that.

"This is Lila," I say, gesturing to the pit bull that's still watching us from behind the bench. "But she's not real friendly."

"Oh."

"She's not mean or anything," I add, feeling the need to defend Lila. "She's just a little shy. It's one reason we're here. I'm fostering her for a dog rescue, so I'm trying to get her socialized. Make her friendlier and stuff. You can try to say hi if you want. She might just ignore you, though."

Shelby lets go of Pilot's collar, and I take a better look at him. He's tall, with these long, skinny legs and big, pointed ears that seem two sizes too big for his head. He's calmed down a bit now, and his long nose is pressed to the ground, like he's caught some kinda scent he's eager to follow.

Shelby walks over to the side of the bench and crouches down, one arm outstretched, palm up, toward Lila. "Hey, Lila," she says. "Hi, puppy. Wanna let me pet you?"

I watch Lila's reaction. She looks at me first, then at Shelby. She takes a small step toward Shelby, just close enough so she can lower her head and sniff the hand Shelby has offered. But then, in true Lila fashion, she takes a step back, turns around, and lies down, facing away from Shelby.

Shelby don't seem too disappointed, though.

"That's all right," she tells Lila, voice confident. "I'll win you over eventually." She stands up and walks around the bench, plopping down on the seat I'd been occupying a few seconds ago, before her dog startled me. "She's real cute."

"She's all right," I say with a shrug.

Pilot lifts his head then, something across the dog park catching his attention, and takes off toward another group of dogs who are playing a game of chase.

"So you said you're training Lila?" Shelby asks.

I nod.

"That's great. I'm training Pilot, too. Well, kinda. He's got his basic training—sit and stay and all that. But sometimes he's not real good at listening, especially when he's real excited, so we're working on that. My dad's been helping me. But I actually think I'm better with dogs than he is. How's training been going with Lila?"

"It's been going okay," I say, slowly moving to sit down on the bench, a couple feet from Shelby. "She's real smart. Just stubborn. But she's gotten a lot better. My sister is a dog trainer so she's been showing me what to do."

"A dog trainer? That's so cool!" Shelby says. "I'd love to

be a dog trainer one day. Hey! You live near here, right? Maybe we could work on training Pilot and Lila together— since you want to get her more comfortable with people and dogs."

"Um . . . maybe," I say.

And honestly—surprisingly—that doesn't sound like too bad an idea. I still ain't sure about this girl. I'm still wondering what she'll think of my cane or of me being blind when it comes up. And she's so upbeat it makes me kinda nervous. But if I'm gonna be stuck here for a while, maybe it'd be nice to make a new friend.

And one good thing about Shelby talking so much is that it means I don't have to. Unlike Beth, Shelby doesn't push me to say much. She's more than happy to just talk about Pilot and the other dogs she's met in the neighborhood. And I'm all right with just listening.

And eventually, I realize we've been at the dog park for more than an hour.

"Oh no," I say, getting to my feet and grabbing Lila's leash. "Sorry. I gotta go. My sister will be home soon."

"That's okay," Shelby says. "I should go, too. Let me round up Pilot, and then we can walk out together."

Shelby hops up and goes to get Pilot, and I pick up Lila's

leash. She's under the bench now, lying on her stomach, and looks to be fast asleep. I shake her awake. She opens one eyelid to look at me.

"Come on," I tell her. "Time to go. Glad you used this trip to the dog park to get a nap in."

Lila wiggles out from under the bench, sits up, and yawns while I hook her leash onto her collar.

Feeling a bit nervous, I grab my cane and start walking toward the gate. Shelby's waiting for me there, and I see her look down at my cane as I get close. I hold my breath, waiting. Knowing she's about to bring it up. Sure she's either gonna tease me or, worse, act like she feels bad for me.

But after hardly a second has passed, she looks up at me, smiling, and just says, "Ready to go?"

"Uh, sure."

Once we're out of the dog park and crossing the street, Shelby says, "I gotta go this way." She gestures in the opposite direction of Beth's house. "But it was real nice meeting you and Lila. Finally. Let's meet up again soon, okay? Do you have a cell phone?"

I hand her my phone, and she puts her number in before handing it back to me.

Glancing down, I see that—to my surprise—Lila is

sniffing at Pilot, who's wagging his tail, clearly loving the attention.

"Come on, Pilot. We'll see our new friends again soon," Shelby says, tugging at the dog's leash. "See you two around!"

I watch her walk away, then look down at Lila. She's watching them, too.

I don't say anything to Lila as we start walking back toward Beth's house. I don't think I need to. I get the feeling we're both feeling the same thing. Nervous, unsure. But, maybe, a tiny bit hopeful, too.

Later that night, I get Lila up on the bed with me and try to take a selfie of us both. It takes a few tries. I ain't real good with selfies since it's hard to see my phone when it's too far from my face. But eventually I get one that's all right. Even if Lila refuses to look right at the camera.

I text the picture to both Joey and Maya.

They stopped texting me about two weeks ago, after a lot of messages I didn't reply to. But I ain't gonna do like Beth. I ain't gonna let so much time pass that I feel too embarrassed or guilty to reach out to them again.

Sorry I've been so hard to get a hold of lately.

I miss y'all.

For a minute, I'm worried they won't respond, that I've been too bad of a friend and now they're mad at me. But both of them send replies within a couple minutes of each other.

We miss you, too! What's Kentucky like?

Whose cute dog is that???? Oh, and yeah—miss you, too!

I smile, first at my phone, then at Lila, before typing out a long overdue message to my friends.

Chapter Sixteen

"So is Shelby your new best friend now?" Joey asks.

It's a couple days later and he, Maya, and I are all on a three-way video call. It's the first time I've heard their voices since I left Tennessee, and I don't think I realized how much I missed them.

"Y'all are still my best friends," I say. "I only just met Shelby. She's nice, though."

"And you said she has a pool," Maya chimes in. "No offense, Joey, but I'd be her best friend, too. Ugh. It's so hot. I wish I had a pool."

"Yeah. In fact, I gotta go in a few minutes. I told her I'd meet her at one o'clock so we can go swimming."

"Just promise you ain't gonna start liking her more than us and go ages without talking to us again," Joey says.

Maya goes quiet.

Slowly, I sit down on my bed, holding my phone in front of my face so they can see me. The sadness in Joey's face when he says this twists my gut. I'd explained over text the other day the truth about Mama and apologized for lying about it to them. I'd told them I'd only been avoiding them because I didn't wanna talk about it and had felt embarrassed and that I'd been sad not to be there with them. They'd been real understanding. They barely even commented on Mama's actions at all, just asked how I was doing with it all. Which was a relief. But now I can see that I'd hurt their feelings a lot, too. Even Maya, though she ain't saying anything, looks away from the camera.

"Y'all," I say quietly, "I promise I ain't gonna do that again. I'm . . . I'm sorry I did that to begin with."

"We thought you'd found people you liked more than us or something. That you didn't like us as much anymore," Joey says. "That you didn't wanna bother talking to us now that you'd moved."

"It wasn't that at all. It wasn't about either of you. It wasn't that I liked anyone better or y'all any less. I just . . . Things have been hard."

"We know," Maya says. "But, Hadley, we're your best friends. We wanna be there to help when things are hard."

I decide I ain't gonna tell them there's nothing they could've done. That won't make them feel any better right now. So instead I just say, "Thank you. I'll . . . I'll remember that for next time."

"Well, hopefully there won't have to be a next time," Joey says. "It sounds like between your dog and the friend with the pool, Kentucky ain't half bad."

"She ain't my dog," I say. "But she's all right." I look over at Lila, who's lying by my bedroom door, next to the bag I've packed for my pool day at Shelby's house. I think she knows I'm going somewhere and is making it real clear I ain't leaving without her. "I ain't really a dog person, but she's a good one."

"We're just glad to have you back," Maya says. "We missed you. It's gonna be weird starting school without you."

"Yeah . . ." I've been trying not to think too hard about that. About what it'll be like going to school without them, in a place where I don't know anyone but Shelby. And, on top of that, with my new cane.

I ain't ready to deal with it yet.

Right then, there's a knock at my bedroom door.

"Hadley," Mrs. McGraw calls. "One of those house flipping shows is on. Do you wanna come watch it with me?"

"I can't," I call through the door. "I gotta go meet Shelby at one. We're gonna go swimming at her house."

"Oooh. I know Shelby. She's a nice girl. Real nice." This ain't surprising. Everybody knows everybody in small towns like these. "But you'd better get going then. It's nearly one o'clock now."

"I know, I know."

"Is that your babysitter?" Maya asks.

I sigh. "Kinda. I guess. I don't need a babysitter, but Beth won't listen. Mrs. McGraw's okay, though. Sometimes."

"Have fun with Shelby," Joey says. "I know I sounded kinda jealous before, but . . . I do hope you make friends."

"Thanks, Joey."

I say goodbye to them both and promise I'll call them again soon. Maya suggests we make a schedule where I gotta talk to them for an hour at least once a week and then text the rest of the time. She likes organizing stuff like that. She even has a calendar on her fridge at home with a list of all her after-school activities and the times of all of them. Joey likes to say she schedules in her fun. Maya says that ain't a bad thing.

I miss them both.

Once I hang up, I grab my bag, my cane, and Lila's leash—she's getting her wish—and the two of us head out of the house and toward the dog park, where Shelby said she'd meet us. I ain't seen her since we exchanged numbers a couple days ago. But she's called and texted a few times and yesterday she said we ought to go swimming at her house.

I feel a bit nervous about it—going to her house when I don't know her real well—but Beth says she knows Shelby's parents and that it's okay. And who am I to turn down the chance to swim in this heat?

Besides, Shelby does seem nice. Maybe it won't hurt to have one friend in this town.

"Hadley!" she calls out when Lila and I round the corner near the dog park. "Over here!"

At her side, Pilot lets out a friendly bark. Like he's greeting us, too.

"I'm so glad you're coming over," Shelby says once Lila and I reach her. "It'll be nice to have some company. Plus, it's so hot. Ugh. I hate it. So does Pilot. He's got too much fur for this weather."

Pilot don't seem too bothered by it right now, though. He's tugging on his leash, hopping all over Lila and me, excited to see us. Lila just sorta lets him. She don't seem quite as happy to see him and Shelby, but she doesn't whine or hide behind me either, so that's something.

"Thanks for inviting me," I say. "It was real nice of you."

"Of course!" Shelby says. "And I'm so happy you could bring Lila. She and Pilot can play in the yard while we swim. We've got a fence around the backyard, so they'll be all right. And my brothers have summer school, so they won't be around to bother us."

Shelby's house is just a block from the dog park in the opposite direction of Beth's. She opens the gate and leads us all inside.

"Take off your shoes if you don't mind," she says, slipping off her own sandals. "And you can take Lila's leash off. Does she like toys? Pilot has a lot of toys. She can play with them if she wants."

Sure enough, Lila's leash ain't off for five seconds before she's found Pilot's tug rope, and the two of them start a game of tug-of-war in Shelby's living room. It's the friendliest I've seen her be with anyone but me so far. I guess her shyness is overcome by the promise of a good game.

Shelby points me in the direction of her bathroom so I can change into my bathing suit. And when I'm done changing and putting on the sunblock I grabbed from Beth's bathroom, I make my way back to her living room, using my cane to be careful not to run into anything. She's waiting for me there, wearing a bright yellow swimsuit and sunglasses.

"Ready to go out to the pool?" she asks. But she opens the back door before I can even answer and calls out, "Daddy! Hadley and Lila are here."

I follow her outside. Pilot and Lila are close behind me, and Lila's still got the tug rope hanging from her mouth. A man—Shelby's dad I guess—is sitting on the pool deck in a lawn chair. When I get closer, I can see that he's wearing a ball cap and he's got a laptop on his knees.

"You must be Hadley," he says. "Nice to meet you. I'm Shelby's dad. Beth's your sister, right?"

I nod.

"She's a good one. We love having her in the neighborhood. She's trained several people's dogs around here. Been thinking of contacting her for some help with Pilot."

"I can train Pilot, Daddy," Shelby protests.

"I'm sure you can," he replies. "The question is, can you do it before Pilot digs up the rest of your mama's garden?"

Shelby lets out an indignant huff. "We're gonna go swimming, okay?"

"That's fine," her dad says. "I'll be right here if you need me. Just working on lesson plans."

"Daddy's a teacher at the high school," Shelby explains as we walk to the edge of the pool. "So he's got the summer off like we do."

"Oh," I say.

And then . . .

"Cannonball!"

Before I can blink, Shelby has taken about three steps back and then sprinted to the edge of the pool, leaping in. Water sprays up onto the deck, splashing me real good in the process. A second later, Shelby surfaces with a laugh.

"Oh man, it's cold," she says. "Should've got in more slowly."

My first instinct is to be irritated about being splashed, but I manage to shake it off. Shelby's been nothing but nice to me so far, and I'm gonna get wet anyway. I don't gotta be upset *all the time*.

I do climb down the ladder slowly, though, because the water is pretty cold.

Once Shelby's gotten used to the water, she starts swimming in circles around me, diving and doing flips beneath the water. She's kinda a show-off, I realize. Me, on the other hand, I mostly just hang out in the middle of the pool, happy enough to float for a bit.

Shelby asks me a ton of questions, but not the ones I expect her to. Nothing about my cane or why I live with Beth. Instead, she wants to know about my old school, about Tennessee, about my friends back home. I tell her about Joey and Maya, and how jealous they are that she has a pool.

Then I figure it's my turn to ask some questions.

"What about your friends?" I ask.

"My friends? Oh, let's see. Well, my two best friends are Cate and Cassie. They're twins. But they spend summers with their grandparents in Georgia, so I ain't seen them in a bit. In person, at least. We'll get on a video call sometimes, but mostly we just text and send each other funny videos we find online."

"So . . . you ain't seen them all summer?"

"Nope," Shelby says, and for the first time, I hear a touch of sadness in her voice. "And I miss them a lot. But that's one reason I was so excited to finally get to talk to you the other day! I was . . . kinda hoping to make a new friend. Summers around here get awful lonely, you know?"

"Well . . . um . . . I guess I'm glad we got to meet, then,"

I say. It sounds awkward coming out of my mouth, but Shelby don't seem to notice.

"Me, too," she says. "And when school starts, you'll get to meet Cate and Cassie! Maybe you can join the middle school book club with us. I promise you'll like them. They don't have any dogs. Their mom's allergic. They'll be so jealous of you getting to have Lila."

"Aren't they jealous of Pilot, then, too?" I ask.

"Not really." Shelby sighs. "I think Pilot is . . . well, a little bit too much for them to handle."

And, as if on cue, I hear Shelby's dad holler, "Pilot, no!" as Pilot bounds up the deck and then—without hesitation— leaps into the swimming pool with Shelby and me.

We both squeal and move away as the fluffy black German shepherd surfaces and begins paddling around.

"Dang it, Pilot," Shelby says. "You *know* you ain't supposed to get in the pool!"

I struggle not to laugh as I say, "I think this might be why your daddy wants to call my sister."

"Maybe, but I can do it on my own! I know how to— Oh no. Here comes Lila."

"Huh?"

I turn around and see Lila standing at the edge of the

pool. She's watching us—Shelby, Pilot, and me—like she's debating what to do.

I know I ought to tell her no, keep her from jumping in like Pilot has, but I'm curious to see what she'll do.

She looks directly at me, then, with only a second's pause, leaps into the water.

Pilot barks, like he's showing his approval as he swims toward her.

"We're gonna have to clean the pool again after this," Shelby whines. But then she starts laughing, and so do I.

The dogs swim around us, splashing and playing. Lila even lets Shelby pet her for a minute before she paddles away after Pilot. It's the most fun I've seen Lila have since I've known her.

It's the most fun *I've* had since I've known her.

When we're done, we gotta get Shelby's daddy's help pulling the dogs out, since they can't climb up the ladder. And Shelby complains again about how dirty the pool is and how she's gotta clean it now.

But I think it was worth it.

Chapter Seventeen

On Thursday evening, when Beth gets home from work, she tells me that Vanessa will be coming over tomorrow for dinner. She says it's to check on Lila, but based on how giggly and nervous she gets when she tells me, I get the feeling it's kinda a date, too. One I'll be stuck in the middle of.

"Are you supposed to be dating your boss?" I ask as I pick up both of our empty plates after dinner and take them to the sink. "Ain't there a rule against it or something?"

"She's not actually my boss. I'm a freelancer. A contractor."

I turn on the faucet and begin rinsing off the dishes. "But didn't you say she hired you?"

"Technically, yes. She offered me a contract. But I work for myself. I'm my own boss. People hire me for my services.

I don't work for the dog rescue, but Vanessa has me under contract to help them with some training. So . . . no, Vanessa's not my boss."

"So you're allowed to date her." I grab the dish soap and a sponge and start washing, eager to get the dishes clean before Beth's phone starts ringing with Mama's call.

"I suppose some people would frown at it, but we've talked about it. And it's something we're both comfortable with. Especially since Right Choice isn't my only client." She stands up from the table and comes to lean against the fridge as she watches me wash the dishes. She folds her arms over her chest. "You know, you're awful interested in my love life."

"Am not."

"Mmm-hmm. You could've fooled me, the way you always ask me questions about it. Any time I bring up Vanessa, you ask about us dating."

"Do not!"

"Do so," Beth says, and I can hear the laughter bubbling beneath her words.

"Ugh. You're so annoying!" I finish scrubbing her plate and shut off the water. "I'm never asking you about it again!" I declare as I storm off to my room. I can hear her laughing behind me as I go.

But the next day, I get up early—well, before noon—and decide it'd be a good idea to give Lila a bath before we have company. Beth's got a bunch of dog brushes and shampoo and stuff in the cabinet under the bathroom sink. I set all of it out on the counter, then go to the kitchen to grab a jar of peanut butter and a knife.

"Hadley?" Mrs. McGraw asks as I trek through the house, gathering up supplies. "What are you up to?"

"Gonna give Lila a bath."

"All right. To tell the truth, she could probably use one. But why do you have peanut butter in your hand?"

I pretend I don't hear her and run back to the bathroom to get started.

By this point, I know Lila well enough to know she ain't gonna make this easy on me. So I did my research and found the perfect way to keep her in the tub while I wash her.

I use the knife to smear peanut butter all over the tiled wall of the tub, right across from the faucet. I'm halfway done before it occurs to me that maybe I ought to have run this idea past Beth, since it's her house and her jar of peanut butter. But too late. When I'm done, I call Lila to me, and just as I'd hoped, she hops right in the tub and starts licking the peanut butter off the wall. That keeps her occupied for quite a while and gives me plenty of time to scrub her with dog shampoo and rinse her off.

Half an hour later, Mrs. McGraw ain't too pleased about the wet pit bull running through the house or me in my soaked clothes, but she does offer to help me dry Lila off.

"You know," she says, "this was a real nice thing for you to do today. Even if Lila is making an awful big mess. Beth will be so tickled you actually did this without her asking."

I just shrug. "It ain't a big deal."

By dinnertime, when Vanessa shows up, Lila's all dry and I've changed into a new pair of jeans and a dry T-shirt. And I gotta say, I'm pretty proud of my handiwork. Lila smells real nice once the wet-dog odor goes away.

Not that Vanessa or Beth are paying much attention to what the dog smells like.

From the minute Vanessa walks in—dressed in a white tank top and skinny jeans, rather than the work clothes I last saw her in—Beth can't take her eyes off her. And I don't think Vanessa minds too much, based on the way she grins at my sister every time Beth says anything to her.

It's kinda cute, I guess, but also pretty annoying, since I gotta sit through dinner with the both of them. I might as well not even be here.

"Beth, this is delicious," Vanessa says, taking a bite of her barbecue chicken sandwich before wiping her mouth on a napkin. "Do you like to cook?"

"Sometimes," Beth says. "But I don't do it as much as I ought to."

"Did your mom teach you?"

"A little bit, but honestly, Daddy was more the cook in our family. He was really good, and really enjoyed cooking, too. I remember Mama saying that once she realized how good he was in the kitchen, she knew she was gonna have to marry him."

"Smart woman," Vanessa says. "My dad's the cook in our family, too. Though Mom still tries. *Tries* being the key word there. She's really bad at it." She laughs, shaking her head. "If you ever meet her, don't tell her I said that. She'd skin me alive."

"I'd love to meet your mother one day."

"And I'd love for you to meet her."

I clear my throat and drop the spoon I'd been eating my mashed potatoes with, letting it clatter onto my plate. Beth and Vanessa both turn to look at me.

"I'm done eating," I say, because I can't handle being a third wheel much longer. "Can I be excused? I'll do the dishes later."

"Uh—" Beth begins.

But Vanessa says, "You know, I'm about done here, too. And I'd love to see what progress you've made with Lila. Why don't you grab her and we'll meet you in the living room in a minute?"

I shrug. "Sure."

I take a handful of baby carrots from the fridge and call Lila into the living room with me.

"Listen," I whisper to her while, in the next room, Vanessa and Beth finish off their food. "Don't be stubborn tonight, okay? Do what I ask, even though people will be watching. Don't make me look silly. Please?"

Lila just sniffs at the hand where I'm hiding her carrots. Her tail does wag, though, so I'm gonna take that as an agreement.

When the phone rings—Mama's nightly call—Beth keeps it quick for once. And, a few minutes later, she and Vanessa are sitting next to each other on the sofa, watching quietly as I run through the different commands I've taught Lila.

"Sit . . . Good! Lie down . . . Good girl. Stay . . . Good. Now, come!"

Lila does it all as if Beth and Vanessa aren't even there. When we've run through everything, I turn to look at our audience while Lila crunches on the last of the baby carrots.

"I'm impressed," Vanessa tells me. "Not surprised, though. I had a good feeling about pairing you two up. And my good feelings are rarely wrong."

"Hadley spends a lot of time with her," Beth says. "She even took Lila to the dog park the other day."

"I don't think she liked that a whole lot, though," I admit. I sit down on the floor so that Lila can come and lie down next to me, putting her big head in my lap. I scratch behind her ears. "She mostly just slept under a bench. But I met a girl there—Shelby—she's got a really friendly dog that Lila gets along with. I think we're gonna try and get them together to work on training stuff at the same time."

"That's great," Vanessa says.

"You know, as fast as Lila's been learning, it makes me wonder if she's been trained before?" Beth says. "If whoever her last owner was had done some work with her. And she just didn't want to do it anymore until Hadley came along and did some practice with her."

"Maybe," Vanessa replies.

"But why would anyone train a dog just to get rid of them?" I ask.

179

"I don't know," Beth admits. "But dogs end up in rescues for all sorts of reasons. It might not be as simple as all that. Most likely we'll never know. But it's just something I've been thinking about. Not to take away from all the work you've been doing, of course! You've still worked miracles with this dog, even if she might've known a few commands before."

"You really have," Vanessa agrees. "Hmm. I know there's still some things to be worked on, but at this rate, I bet we can have Lila adopted out by the end of the summer."

My stomach drops. "That . . . That soon?"

"Sure. I don't see why not."

But I can think of a lot of reasons *why not*.

I've known from the start that Lila ain't my dog, that I am only training her so she can find a permanent home. But somehow, for the last few weeks, that's seemed like something real far away. So far away it was hardly worth considering.

The end of the summer, though . . . that's not far away. Not at all.

I look down at Lila. Her eyes are open, and she's staring back up at me. I try to imagine what it'd be like being here in Beth's house without her. But the thought is so lonely I can't take it.

"Just give it a few more weeks of that good work you've been doing with her," Vanessa continues, oblivious to the sadness washing through me, "and we'll be able to put her picture up on the website. She'll be in a good forever home in no time. And it'll all be thanks to you, Hadley."

"Yeah," I mumble, heart squeezing hard in my chest. "Thanks to me."

I feel like a real fool. Because somehow, I hadn't realized that in helping Lila get better, I might be breaking my own heart.

Beth must be able to guess how I'm feeling. She don't say nothing while Vanessa's here, but she comes knocking on my bedroom door later that night.

"Hey," she says, as she cracks the door open. "You still up?"

"Yeah."

I'm lying on my bed with Lila curled up on the other side of me. We're both under the covers, and she's started hogging my pillow. I don't fight her, though.

"Good," Beth says. "Y'all scoot over."

"Huh?"

"Scoot."

She turns on the bedside lamp before giving my arm a light shove with her hand. I scoot over a little and push Lila a bit closer to the edge of the bed so I've got room. She gives an irritated huff before rolling onto her side so that her legs are stretched across me.

Beth sits on the now empty side of the bed. For a second, I think she's gonna try and talk to me about what Vanessa said, about Lila finding a real home. I think she's gonna remind me that she never said we could keep a dog right now and that this was always the plan, and it's best for Lila so I gotta be okay with it. I've got this whole annoying speech in my head that I'm sure my sister's about to give me.

But instead, she pulls out a book. I can't read the title from here—the light is far too dim for my eyes—but I can hear the pages turning as she cracks the spine.

"What's that?" I ask.

"A book."

I scowl at her. "I figured that. What book?"

"One of my favorites. I stopped by that bookshop I told you about the other day and picked up a copy." She leans back against the headboard and flips the pages a second before saying, "Here we go. *The Giver* by Lois Lowry. Chapter One—"

"Beth, you ain't gotta do this," I tell her. "I don't need you to read to me."

"I know," Beth says. "Now shhh. Ahem. Chapter One . . ."

I lie there quietly for about an hour, listening to Beth read. She's not as theatrical about it as Mama always was. She don't do the voices or anything like that. But it's still a pretty interesting story, even without the sound effects.

My bed really ain't big enough for two girls and a pit bull, but squished there, between Beth and Lila, I'm able to pretend—just for a minute—that everything's gonna be okay. That I could be happy here, with my sister and Lila. That the end of summer is a long way off, and I ain't gotta think about Lila going anywhere anytime soon. I'm able to tell myself I ain't got nothing to worry about.

For a minute, I think I understood why Mama lied, why she'd said things were gonna be okay even when they weren't.

Because right now, trying to believe my own lie is a whole lot easier than facing the truth.

Chapter Eighteen

As we near the end of July, Shelby calls me almost every day. Sometimes she just wants to chat. Other times she asks if we can meet up and take our dogs for a walk or swim at her house again. I always say yes. Ain't like I got anything better to do.

She likes to talk a lot. Sometimes when we're walking, she'll go on for a long while about a book or a movie she watched, or tell me about the trouble her siblings get into. I don't mind. It's kinda nice to just listen and not be expected to answer all the time. And when she does ask me questions, she seems real interested in the answer, even if I don't say a whole lot.

She never brings up my cane or how sometimes it's obvious I can't see things.

So, eventually, I do it for her.

"You know I'm blind, right?"

I blurt it out on one of our walks around the neighborhood. Lila and Pilot are on their leashes, walking in front of Shelby and me. Lila's really warmed up to Pilot. She gets all excited when she first sees him, and she don't even seem to mind when he jumps all over her or sniffs her butt. Dogs are so weird. Anyway, she's even started sparing a tail wag or two for Shelby, who seems real pleased by this, considering how Lila ignored her the first day they met.

Shelby was in midsentence, talking about some TV show her little brother made her watch, when I interrupted her. I feel bad for a second, knowing cutting her off like that was rude, but she don't seem bothered about it as she turns her head to look at me fully.

"Yeah," she says after a second. "I figured."

"Not completely blind," I explain. "Not yet. Maybe not ever. But it will get worse, doctors say. I used to be able to see all right but now . . . Well, now I gotta use this thing." I tap the cane on the concrete as we make our way down the sidewalk, past a little grocery store. "So yeah. I'm . . . *legally blind* is what they call it. I can still see, but not . . . not real well."

Shelby nods. "Okay."

"You . . . You ain't said anything about it."

"Neither have you."

"I know, but . . ."

"I figured if you wanted to talk about it, you'd bring it up," she says. "And now you have, so . . . do you wanna talk about it?"

"No," I say quickly, and then, "Maybe? I don't really know. I didn't wanna talk about it for a while because . . . because I thought talking about it made it more real, and I didn't want it to be. That's stupid, though. And now I got this cane, and that makes it feel more real, too." I shake my head. "I guess . . . I guess I just don't know what to say. Other than that it sucks. And it's . . . kinda scary. My mobility teacher—the lady who's teaching me to use this cane—says it'll be easier once I know how to do all the stuff she's teaching me. And just things like walking around like this have gotten a bit easier, I suppose. But . . . still." I look down at the sidewalk. My cane sweeps, scratching across the concrete in time with my steps. I barely notice any sort of ache in my wrist now. And I haven't jabbed myself in the belly with the end in a few days. "I'm sorry," I mutter.

"For what?" Shelby asks.

"Going on and on about this. I know it ain't fun to hear."

"I don't mind," she says. "I can't say if things will get easier or better or whatever, because I ain't been in your shoes before. Closest I got is an uncle who's completely blind."

"Really?"

"Yeah. He was in the military. Lost his sight in an explosion, I think."

"That's awful."

"He had a hard time with it at first. Was just real angry that it happened. But he's doing all right now. He's got one of those dogs that helps him out—a guide dog, I think he called it. She's real cute. He ended up going to culinary school and is a chef at a fancy restaurant in Lexington now."

"How does he read recipes?"

"He has them made in Braille. Or he has this thing on his phone so it'll read out stuff to him. It's in a kinda robot voice, but he don't seem to mind that."

"How does he use the oven or the stove? How does he measure stuff?" I ask as a dozen other questions run through my mind. I can barely see a lot of that kinda stuff now, and I ain't completely blind yet.

"I ain't sure about all that," Shelby admits. "I know his kitchen is real organized, and he has come up with ways to make it work for him, though. He's a good cook. Grandma started insisting we have Thanksgiving at his house instead of hers so he can cook for all of us. Mmm. Now I'm hungry." She chuckles. "Anyway. I don't think it was easy for him or anything. But he's doing all right. I don't know if it'll be the same for you. I hope so, of course, but . . . I don't mind listening if you want me to. Sorry if that ain't much help."

"No, I appreciate it," I tell her. "Everybody else—my sister and my teacher—they all wanna talk about it just to tell me it's gonna get easier. And maybe they're right. But sometimes I don't wanna hear two people who ain't been through this tell me how it's gonna be. I just wanna be upset a little. Even if it does get easier—even if I end up doing real well like your uncle—it still stinks *right now.*"

"My mama calls that venting," Shelby says. "When she gets home after a bad day and tells my dad about it, sometimes he tries to make suggestions for how to fix things, and it just gets her madder. She says sometimes people just gotta vent."

"Why's it called venting?"

"No idea," Shelby says. "Just what she calls it. So if you ever gotta vent to me, go right ahead."

"Thank you," I say.

I turn my eyes back to Lila and Pilot, still walking just

ahead of us, leashes a little loose. Now that Pilot's gotten used to me and Lila being around, he's actually doing pretty good on the leash. I've got this theory that he and Lila are trying to impress each other, because sometimes as they walk, one of the dogs will look over at the other for a minute and then wag their tail. It's pretty cute, if I'm being honest.

We decide to go to the dog park for a little bit to let the dogs run around before we separate and head back to our houses. As soon as we're inside the fence and we've taken their leashes off, Lila and Pilot start racing around the dog park.

Lila still don't play with the other dogs much—just Pilot—but at least she ain't hiding behind the bench anymore.

Shelby and I find an empty seat in the shade. And after we've been sitting for a minute, I say, "Can I tell you something?"

"Sure. What?"

"When I saw you that day at the picnic tables—I realized you were staring at me. And, at first, I got real upset. Because I thought you were looking at me because of my cane. I thought you were gonna tease me about it or something."

"Really?" Shelby asks, clearly surprised. And maybe a little hurt. "That'd be awful. I'd never do that."

"I know that now," I say. "I was real relieved when I met you here and realized you were only staring because you wanted to be friends with my dog."

"And you."

"Mostly my dog."

"Well, maybe."

We both laugh, and I try to ignore the fact that I've just referred to Lila as "my dog" even though she ain't mine at all. Even though Vanessa says it probably won't be long before we can find her a real home. I shake off the thought. It was just a slip of the tongue. I know she ain't mine. And I got other things I'm worrying about right now.

"Shelby," I say, "do you think people at your school will tease me about it?"

"About you being almost blind?"

"Yeah." I fidget with Lila's leash, which I'm still holding in my hands. "I'm gonna be living with my sister for a while, so I'll probably be going to your school when it starts up in a few weeks. No one at my old school really made fun of me about it. But I didn't use a cane. And also I'd known everyone there since kindergarten. So my vision getting worse slowly like it has wasn't as big a deal to them. And . . . I'm just nervous about being made fun of, I guess."

Shelby takes a minute to answer. When she does, she says, "I don't know. I wanna believe they wouldn't. Most people at school are pretty nice. I know my friends, Cate and Cassie, wouldn't, but . . . I can't say for sure, Hadley. I'm sorry."

"Yeah . . ."

"But." She touches my arm and waits to speak until I've looked over at her. When I do, she's staring back at me, real direct. "If anybody does act like jerks, just let me know. And I'll kick their butts." She lifts her arm and flexes it with a grin.

I can't help but laugh. The idea of Shelby—with her pig-tails and her big smile—fighting anyone is pretty silly. But it does cheer me up a bit.

"Thanks," I say.

"Anytime."

Later, when Lila and I are walking back to Beth's house, I can't help but think that it's interesting: Shelby didn't try to make any promises about how things would get better or easier. Or try to tell me she understood what I was going through or any of that stuff people often do when they know I'm losing my sight. But she also didn't act like she pitied me, either. Instead, she just offered to let me talk, and promised to be there for me if I needed her to.

To my own surprise, I believe her.

And, for the first time in a while, I do actually feel a little better—a little less angry and afraid—about what'll happen in the future. At least where me and my eyes are concerned.

Chapter Nineteen

It's the end of July, only a couple weeks before the start of the school year, when Cilia gives me my biggest challenge yet. She'd warned me at our last lesson, while the younger kids were packing up their things, that the next session would be one-on-one and that, instead of meeting me at the community center, she'd be picking me up from Beth's house.

So on Monday afternoon, Mrs. McGraw—with Lila's leash in hand—waves me off as I climb into Cilia's minivan. I shut my door and buckle my seat belt before turning to look at my teacher. "So where we going?"

"Not too far," she answers, backing out of the short driveway. "You've been doing well with your cane technique, and you picked up on street crossing methods really fast. So I thought today I'd give you a bit more of a challenge."

I ain't sure what that means, and if I'm being honest, it makes me a little nervous. But I don't got a lot of time to think about it because Cilia only drives for a couple minutes before parking the car and cutting the engine.

We're on a busy street—well, as busy as any of the streets around here seem to get—with cars parked on either side. There are several buildings, too, clustered close together, but I can't tell what they are. Shops or offices or something. We must be downtown.

"Okay," Cilia says, undoing her seat belt and swiveling to reach into the back seat. She grabs something that looks like a binder before easing back into the driver's seat. "So today I'm going to have you go on a route. But we're going to do it a little differently than usual. Instead of walking close behind you and directing you where to go, I'm going to make a map for you to memorize. I'll be walking behind you at a distance, but I won't be saying anything unless you really need help. The goal is for you to feel like you're doing this on your own."

"Okay," I say. "I guess. But you're forgetting one big thing."

"What's that?"

"I'm not gonna be able to see a map real well, I don't think."

"I didn't forget," Cilia says. She opens the binder and places it in my lap.

On one side of the open binder there's a sheet of black Velcro. On the other, there's a zipped pocket filled with various thin pieces of plastic. I ain't sure what the heck this is supposed to be, even when Cilia unzips the pocket and shows me that the plastic pieces—most of which are long, thin rectangles—have Velcro on the back.

"What's this?"

"This is how I'm going to make a map," Cilia explains. "One you can see, but also feel if you need to. These pieces will be streets. I'll lay out the route here, then give you a couple minutes to memorize it before we get started."

Cilia walks me through placing the plastic pieces onto the Velcro sheet, letting the long, thin pieces serve as the path I'm meant to take. She even has me put little spaces between the pieces to show where I'll need to cross a street. And when we're done, I'm holding a sort of 3-D map I can run my fingers over as I try to memorize the several turns I'll have to make, which will eventually lead back to my starting point, near the van. And, according to Cilia, right in front of the best ice cream shop in town.

"I know this might seem silly," Cilia admits. "You have a cell phone and you can probably pull up a map on there and even have the phone give you directions with the voice-over function. We'll do a route like that at some point, if you want, but there are going to be times where that might not be an option. Maybe your phone is dead or you don't have signal or Wi-Fi. So it's always a good idea to have a route in mind before you go somewhere alone. Since you can't see street signs, you'll have to know exactly where you're going. Counting street crossings and stuff like that. Making a route like this—something you can memorize by touching it if you want—is always an option."

"Right." But my stomach is tying itself in knots. I've done a lot of walking around Beth's neighborhood, but it's always been with her or Shelby. The farthest I've had to walk alone is to the dog park, and that's mostly a straight shot from Beth's house. Not a lot to remember.

As if she can sense my worry, Cilia says, "Like I said, I'll be walking behind you. If there's any chance you're in danger or if it seems like you're struggling, I'll be right here to help. Just take a couple more minutes to get a feel for it, and we'll get started."

I run my hands over the plastic pieces, trying to learn the map both visually and tactilely. My lips move around the words as I say the route to myself a few times. "Two blocks up. Turn left. Three blocks. Turn right . . ."

But eventually Cilia gently takes the binder from my lap and closes it, tucking it under her arm. "All right," she says, popping open her door. "Let's get started."

I climb out of the minivan and unfold my cane while I wait for Cilia to come around. She meets me on the sidewalk and gives me an encouraging smile—which honestly just makes me feel irritated because it's more pressure if I mess up—before sending me off.

The first block is easy, of course. I just gotta walk straight down the sidewalk to the curb. I try and focus on my cane—on keeping the sweeps in step with my feet, on catching myself once it gets caught in cracks to avoid stabbing myself in the belly. This really ain't so different from walking in Beth's neighborhood.

But then I reach the first street crossing, and this is real different from Beth's neighborhood. Because Beth's neighborhood ain't got a lot of traffic, but we're downtown today, and even though this ain't a big town, there are still more cars here than where Beth lives. I can hear them all whooshing by, but watching for them is hard since my vision is so tunneled now.

I've crossed busier streets than this before, but only with someone else telling me when it was safe to go. Or with Cilia, who taught me how to do it safely but was still always right near me when I did it. Now Cilia's way behind me, and I'm on my own.

Don't make this a big deal, Hadley, I scold myself. *She taught you how to do this. It ain't that hard.*

I turn to watch and listen to the traffic at my left. It's running north, the same direction I'm walking. Once it starts moving, that'll mean it's safe for me to cross because the cars heading east and west won't be able to go through the intersection. Cilia always tells me it's okay to use what vision I got left, but to trust my ears more. So I do. And when it sounds like the first car is about halfway through the intersection— so I know it ain't gonna turn—I start walking.

I gotta fight the urge to run through the crosswalk, to get to safety faster. But I know if I do that, I might trip over my cane, which really ain't meant for jogging, so I walk. Fast. And when I reach the other side, I feel a huge sense of relief.

At least until I remember that, based on the route Cilia made me map, there are about twelve more to go before this is over.

But really, it ain't quite as scary after that. As time goes by, I'm focusing more on remembering the rest of the route than I am on being nervous. About halfway through, I stop at a corner because I can't remember if I was supposed to keep going straight or turn.

"Dang it," I mutter, trying to remember. I know I've gone two blocks since that last turn. I've been counting streets like Cilia taught me. But I'm completely blanking on what I was supposed to do next.

I take a deep breath and close my eyes for a second, trying to remember the little plastic pieces on the Velcro. I imagine running my hands over it the way I had, tracing it with my fingertips. I follow the route from the starting point, remembering all the crossings and turns, right up until I reach where I am now and . . .

Straight. One more block straight and then I turn again.

I keep moving.

It takes me about half an hour to walk the full route. Which ain't real fast—I probably could have done it better—but I know it ain't about speed. And in all the time, I didn't get lost or run over by a car or even have to stop and holler to Cilia for help. I did it completely on my own.

And I only jabbed myself in the belly with my cane three or four times!

So when I reach the place where we started, I've actually

got a smile on my face. And when Cilia catches up, I think she notices.

"You did it!" Cilia says to me. "Nice work!"

I know it seems like a silly thing to feel so proud of—I just took a thirty-minute walk by myself—but I do. It's left me feeling energetic and excited, wanting to map out paths on my own.

"That one street crossing was kinda hard," I admit. "The T-shaped one? That took me a minute."

"I know, but I knew you had it under control," Cilia says. "And now that you've done this once, we'll get more practice soon, with longer routes and different types of street crossings. But for today, you did a very good job, Hadley."

"Thanks."

"And now," she says, looking past me at the ice cream shop. "We still have a bit of time before I need to get you back home. What do you say we grab some ice cream?"

After Cilia and I each eat our cones of ice cream and step back outside, I pass her my phone and ask if she wouldn't mind taking a picture of me.

"Sure," she says.

I take a few steps away from her, then strike a real cute

pose. With my cane held out in front of me. Right there for the camera to see.

When we're back in the van, I look at the picture. I hesitate for a minute before taking a deep breath and posting it.

Hadleybean13: I got a new fashion accessory.
And it's actually kinda useful, too.

I feel anxious about sharing it as soon as I hit post. I'm still nervous about people making fun of me or feeling sorry for me for having to use it. But, after the last few weeks—and today especially—I can't deny it's helpful. I'm still pretty scared about the future, about what's gonna happen as my vision gets worse, but . . .

But today I feel a little *less* scared, I guess.

I gotta accept that the cane is just gonna be a big part of my life now and probably forever. I ain't gonna be able to hide it, and I shouldn't have to. So might as well let everyone see it on my terms, I guess.

We ain't even back to Beth's house when my phone buzzes with notifications from Joey and Maya commenting on the picture.

MayaFairLady: You're so cute, @Hadleybean13! I miss you so much! When you come back to visit will you show us how you use it?

babykangaroo42: You look kinda awesome holding that thing! Also are you allowed to trip people with it? (Just kidding lmao)

babykangaroo42: Come visit us, @Hadleybean13!

And then, a few minutes after that, Shelby comments, too.

ShelzBellz: So stylish! This picture would ONLY be better if Lila was in it with you. Ha-ha.

I type out a quick reply. Well, not "quick" because seeing the phone is hard and it takes me forever to type things out, but still.

Hadleybean13: Thanks, y'all. So glad I have friends like you.

Once we get back to Beth's house, I say goodbye to Cilia and hop out of the van, hurrying up the sidewalk and to the front door. I'm so happy about how the lesson went that I'm not paying attention, so I don't notice that Beth's car is in the driveway, even though she isn't supposed to be home yet. Instead, I just bound up the steps and push open the door, assuming I'll find Mrs. McGraw and Lila waiting for me inside.

But it ain't Mrs. McGraw sitting on the couch when I walk into the living room. It's my sister. Her long blonde hair is pulled back, and she's still wearing her work clothes while she reads something on her phone.

"Hey, Beth," I say. Lila runs up to me, tail wagging, and I kneel down to scratch behind her ears. "You're home early."

"Yeah . . ." Beth sets her phone aside. She hesitates for a second before asking, "How was your lesson?"

"Good," I say. "Real good, actually. Cilia helped me make this raised map, and I did this route by myself. Well, she was behind me, but I was mostly by myself. Anyway, I did pretty well."

"That's great, Hadley," Beth says, but she sounds a little distracted, and it makes me deflate a little.

"Something wrong?"

"No. Not at all," Beth says. "I just . . . Come sit down a second. I wanna talk to you about something."

Every muscle in my body tenses up. I don't like it when grown-ups tell me they wanna talk about something. Last time it happened, Mama told me she'd be going to jail.

"What is it?"

"Come sit down, Hadley."

"No," I say, my hands frozen behind Lila's ears. Lila butts at me with her head, wanting me to keep petting. "Tell me what's going on."

Beth sighs. "Okay. It's good news, actually. About Lila. We think we've found her a home."

Chapter Twenty

My hands fall away from Lila as I stare back at my sister. "You . . . Lila . . . Wait, what?"

Beth sets her phone aside and folds her hands in her lap. "Vanessa felt so confident in all the work you've been doing with Lila that she went ahead and put her picture up on the rescue's website," she explains. And she's doing that thing with her voice again, where it goes all soft, like she's talking to a little kid. "She didn't put up any of her information yet or anything. Just a note that she'd be available for adoption soon. But someone called the rescue today."

"Why does that matter if she ain't ready to be adopted yet?" The words come out forceful and angry. "I'm still training her. I'm still—"

"I know," Beth says. "I know, Hadley. And normally

Vanessa would have just told the person that. Asked them to wait awhile. But the person who called . . . she thinks Lila is her dog."

"I don't understand."

Beth slides off the couch and comes to sit on the floor with Lila and me, her legs folded. She reaches out and strokes Lila's back. Lila doesn't move away from her. Instead, her tail thumps against the floor. And I realize just how much she really has changed since we brought her here.

"The woman who called the rescue recognized Lila's picture," Beth says. "She thinks Lila is her dog. Or *was* her dog. She misses her, and she wants her back."

"And Vanessa is just gonna give her back?" I demand.

"She's going to meet her first. And she wants us to come to the rescue to meet her, too. With Lila. To see how Lila reacts to her."

"Why is she giving her a chance at all?" My voice is loud now. Almost yelling. I don't wanna be, but I can't help it. My chest feels tight and my hands are shaking.

"Hadley . . ."

"Lila ended up in a shelter," I say. "Because y'all got her out of the shelter, right? That's how she got to Right Choice.

But how'd she wind up in a shelter to begin with? If this woman wants her back, she never should've lost her in the first place."

"I don't think she gave Lila up on purpose," Beth says. She's still petting Lila, but her other hand reaches out to touch my shoulder. I jerk away. My sister sighs. "Vanessa had a long talk with her today. She had the same question as you. It sounds like Michelle—that's the woman's name—went through . . . a hard time. She had to go away for a while, and Lila got taken to the shelter. But Michelle is doing better now, and she's been looking for Lila for some time."

"Had to go away to where?"

Beth runs a hand through her hair. "I normally wouldn't tell you this, but Michelle was very open about it, and Vanessa got her permission to share after she explained where Lila was." Still, she hesitates for a minute before answering. "Michelle was arrested about a year ago. She went to jail. Lila was with her when it happened, so the police took Lila to a shelter. And then Right Choice took her in a few months later."

"No."

"No what?"

"She can't have Lila back."

"Hadley, I know you love Lila. And you've done a real good job with her. But we can't keep her."

"That ain't the point," I snap. But maybe it is. Just a little. "This lady went to jail. People go to jail because they've done something *wrong*. Something bad. Why should she get Lila back if she did something bad enough to go to jail?"

"People mess up sometimes. And sometimes they try really hard to make up for it and do better," Beth says softly. "Vanessa says Michelle seems to have gotten her life together. And she loves Lila and misses her a whole lot."

"She should've thought about that before she messed up, then," I mutter. "It's too late. Y'all can't give her back to this lady."

"We want what's best for Lila. Vanessa and I aren't just gonna hand her over without making sure it's the right thing to do. Which is why Vanessa wants all of us to come to the rescue to meet her this Saturday."

"I ain't doing it."

"Yes, Hadley, you are." She reaches out and puts her hand on my shoulder again, and when I try to jerk away, she tightens her grip, just slightly. I look up at her. "You love Lila, right?"

I try to shrug, but even as I do, I can't help answering truthfully. "Yeah."

"Then think about it from Lila's perspective," Beth suggests. "She might really love Michelle, and she might miss her a lot. If it turns out Michelle could have a good home for her, doesn't Lila deserve to be with her again?"

I look down at Lila, whose head is resting in my lap now. She's staring up at me with those big, dark eyes. They look almost concerned. And I'm annoyed to realize I'm having to blink back tears.

"How do you know this lady really cares about her, though?" I ask. My voice comes out choked. "If she messed up bad enough to get arrested and get taken away from Lila, how do you know she really cares about her? And what if it happens again?"

"I can understand why that's something you're afraid of, but sometimes people do learn from their mistakes," Beth says. Her hand on my shoulder is gentle now. "You can meet her this weekend. I promise you, Hadley, if Vanessa or I— even for a second—think Michelle won't take care of Lila or that Lila won't be happy with her, we won't just hand her over. We want Lila to be happy. And we have to give her that chance to be. You love her. You've been so good for her. And I know you want her to be happy."

"If . . . if she's awful, you won't make Lila go?"

"Of course not."

"And if she is okay . . . does that mean Lila will just leave with her? This weekend?"

"No," Beth says. "It won't be that quick. Vanessa is going to interview her and do a home visit—make sure she's got enough space for Lila and all that. And then we're going to meet her, make sure she and Lila get along. Make sure Lila seems like she'll be happy with her. And if all that goes well, there will still be paperwork to do. Lila will stay with us for a few more days while we wrap things up."

I nod, but I don't say nothing. I'm pretty sure if I do, I won't be able to stop myself from bawling.

"It's gonna be okay, Hadley."

But I ain't so sure she's right about that.

"Okay," Beth says, giving Lila one last pet before pushing herself to her feet. "Why, um . . . why don't I heat up some of those leftover pulled pork sandwiches? I know it's a bit early for dinner but . . . but yeah. I'm gonna make us sandwiches, okay?"

I don't answer. I don't think Beth expects me to. I keep

my head down and listen to her footsteps as she walks into the kitchen. My eyes stay on Lila's face. She's still staring back at me.

I lean down and press my face against the top of Lila's head and wrap my arms around her.

And then I stop trying to hold back the tears.

I just let myself cry into Lila's fur.

Chapter Twenty-One

I barely say a word to Beth on Saturday morning. She tries to talk to me over breakfast, but I can't bring myself to do anything besides shrug or nod. Eventually, she gives up, and after I feed Lila, the three of us climb into my sister's car and head to the rescue.

Vanessa is waiting for us outside, by the front door. She smiles and gives Beth a kiss on the cheek before saying, "Michelle's already here. We were just chatting by the dog run around back."

"And?" Beth asks. I can tell she's nervous. But hopeful, too. It makes me feel sick to my stomach.

"And she seems really sweet," Vanessa says. "She's excited to see Lila. I did warn her, of course, that there's a chance she's mistaken and this isn't her dog. And even if it is, that

Lila's not the most outgoing. She might not remember her or be excited to see her. She says she understands all that, though."

"Good," Beth says.

Vanessa turns to me. "How are you, Hadley?"

I shrug and look away.

My sister clears her throat. "Vanessa, we should probably just . . ."

"Ah. Right. Well, follow me, then. She's waiting for us around back."

My right hand clenches around the handle of my cane and my left grips Lila's leash real tight as we follow Vanessa around the side of the building. Behind the dog rescue, there's a huge fenced-in area. Kinda like the dog park near Beth's house, but a whole lot bigger. My guess is that they bring some of the dogs out here to play and get exercise, but right now it looks and sounds pretty empty. Vanessa opens the gate and gestures us inside.

That's when I hear her voice. A woman's voice, soft and nervous, calling out, "Lila?"

Lila sees her before I do. I know because her tail starts wagging and she starts pulling on the leash, harder than she has in ages. So hard that I can't keep hold, and she's tugged herself free of my grip before I can even see who she's running toward.

I see the woman right as Lila barrels into her outstretched arms.

She's got pasty white skin and bright orange-red hair that falls around her shoulders in wild, big curls. Even though she's crouched down, I can tell she ain't real tall. Maybe my height. She's too far for me to make out much else. Not that I need to. I can see the important part.

Lila is jumping all over her, tail wagging, paws flying everywhere. She's yipping and whimpering and just . . . acting like I've never seen Lila act before. I stand there, staring, without a single word to say.

After a minute, Lila breaks away from the redheaded woman—Michelle, I'm guessing—and runs over to me, leash still dragging behind her. She hops up, paws tapping my chest for just a second, before she lands on the ground again and takes off toward Michelle once more. Like she's saying, "Hadley! Did you see? Look who's here!"

When she runs back into Michelle's arms, I can hear the young woman saying, "Lila . . . Lila, I missed you. Good girl. Good, sweet girl," in a broken and croaky voice. She's crying.

And she ain't the only one.

"I guess she does remember you," Beth says. When I look over at her, she's wiping her eyes and Vanessa's arm is around her.

"I think she does," Michelle says. She stands up, but it takes some effort with Lila doing her best to climb into her lap. Even once she's standing, the dog keeps running around her legs, jumping and whining. Like she's happy-crying the way Michelle and Beth are.

I ain't crying, though. I don't feel happy, either. I feel hollow.

"I'm Michelle," the young woman says as she stumbles toward us, tripped by Lila and her dragging leash. "Sorry. I should've introduced myself. I just got a little distracted."

"No, no. That's understandable," my sister replies. "I'm Beth. I do some work training the dogs here. And this is my baby sister, Hadley. We've been—"

"You're the ones who've been fostering Lila, right? Vanessa told me. It's real nice to meet y'all." She turns to look at me, still wiping her eyes. "She, uh . . . Vanessa says you're the one who's really been takin' good care of my girl. Thank you. It means a lot to know Lila was so well loved."

"No thanks to you," I mutter.

"Hadley!" Beth scolds.

"No, no," Michelle says. "I get it. You probably wanna know how Lila ended up in a shelter."

"I already know," I say, and I ain't trying to hide the bitterness in my voice. "You went to jail—because you did something bad—and you left her alone."

"That's not entirely wrong, no. But . . . Why don't we sit down?"

"Michelle," Beth says, "you don't have to explain—"

"No. I do," Michelle replies. "If I was in Hadley's boat and someone just showed up claiming a dog I cared about was theirs, I'd want to know answers. Besides . . . it ain't something I'm gonna bother lying about." She turns back to me. "Come on. Let's, um . . . Let's go sit down over here to talk. There's a bench in the shade."

I almost tell her no. Tell her I don't want her stupid answers. But when I look down, there's Lila, still running around Michelle's legs, still wagging her tail. She's a completely different dog. A happier one. All because Michelle is here.

"Fine," I say. "We can talk."

Vanessa and Beth decide to stay at a distance while Michelle and I take our seats on the bench at the edge of the dog run. I keep my eyes on my feet the whole time, glad for my tunnel vision for once. I don't wanna look at anyone right now.

"So, where do I start?" Michelle says.

I shrug.

"Well, I got Lila a few years back. I was living in an apartment, and the minute I found out they allowed pets, I went out and adopted a little pit bull puppy from a shelter. I guess they'd found Lila's mama and her litter under the porch of an abandoned house? That's what they told me, at least. Lila was only a couple months old. And she was this happy, adorable puppy. I fell in love with her immediately. And at first, things were all right. It was just the two of us."

I try and imagine Lila like that—a happy, excitable little puppy. If you'd described her like that to me a few days ago, I would've been sure you were lying. But now, after the way I've seen her act today with Michelle, I can almost picture it. A tiny puppy running around with a toy—probably a tug rope—hanging out of her mouth, tripping over paws that are still too big for her body, staring at you with eyes that are still too big for her head, that's not quite yet massive like it will be one day.

I wish I'd known her back then.

"But then . . . a year or so after that . . . things weren't so good," Michelle continues. "The company I was working for went bankrupt and had to close down, so I lost my job. And I was having trouble finding a new one. Then my landlord raised the rent on my apartment, so I couldn't afford to live there anymore. I wasn't on good terms with my grand-parents at the time—they're the ones who raised me—so I didn't think I could ask them for help. Everything just sorta tumbled down at once. And, before I knew it, Lila and I were pretty much living out of my car."

Lila has finally calmed down now. She flops onto the ground, stretching across both mine and Michelle's feet. My narrow field of vision is focused right on her wagging tail.

"I kept trying to look for a job, but when you don't got a real address, that's hard. And it just . . . It wasn't getting easier." I can hear Michelle swallow, loud, before she goes on. "The reason I got arrested is because I got caught shop-lifting. I was trying to steal some food for Lila and me. The manager called the police, and I was arrested. At the time, I didn't have anyone I could call to come take her. So the police officer said they'd have to put her in a shelter." Michelle sniffles. I figure she's probably crying now. "I told them her name was Lila, and to make sure the people at the shelter knew it so when I got out, I'd be able to find her easier. But I had no idea how long that would be or if they'd even let me take her back."

"So you went to jail for stealing," I say. My voice is flat. Cold.

"Yeah," Michelle answers. "Trying to, at least. It was wrong. I went about things the wrong way. But I . . . Lila was all I had at that point. I wanted to take care of her. I didn't want either of us to go hungry."

"But you sure weren't taking care of her after you got arrested."

"I know."

"She was probably in that shelter feeling lonely. And scared. And missing you. And mad at you for messing up so bad you had to leave her." I grit my teeth and squeeze my eyes shut tight. Because now I'm the one starting to cry.

"I'm sure she was," Michelle says. "And believe me, if I had it to do over again, I would. I'd do it real different. I'd find some other way. But at the time, I was panicked and worried about taking care of the both of us. It was a stupid decision. But . . . But I've been working to make things better."

"How?"

"Well, I wasn't in jail very long, but while I was there, I did reach out to my grandparents. It wasn't easy, but we started working on mending our fences. We'd had a falling out years before because of a guy I was dating that they didn't like. Turns out they'd been right, but I was stubborn and so were they. But after everything fell apart, it made us all put things into perspective, I guess. So once I was released, I went to live with them. They helped me find a new job, and once I got a little more stable, they helped me find a new place to live. It's taken some time and patience, but I'm in a good spot now. I've tried to learn from the mistakes I've made."

"What about Lila?"

"I started looking for her the day I got out of jail," Michelle tells me. "I contacted the police department to find out what shelter they'd taken her to. But by the time I got in touch with the shelter, she was already gone. And I had no way of knowing what other shelter or rescue she was in or if she'd been adopted by somebody else. All I could do was keep looking. I figured it was a long shot of ever finding her, but I couldn't . . . I couldn't just give up, you know?"

"How long have you been looking for her?" I ask.

"At least a year now," Michelle says.

My eyes are still closed, but I feel two heavy paws press into the tops of my thighs and a warm wet tongue begin to lap at my cheeks. I open my eyes and find myself nose-to-nose with Lila. I reach up and scratch behind her ears.

"I'm okay," I mumble to her. "Thank you, Lila."

Lila licks the tip of my nose before pushing off my lap and going back over to Michelle. She sits right in front of her, looking up at her with big eyes that ain't so sad anymore. Her mouth even hangs open a little, making it look like she's smiling.

"She loves you," I say to Michelle. "It's real obvious."

Michelle laughs as she reaches down to rub Lila's head. "She's a good girl. I love her, too."

And, despite everything, I believe her.

She did something bad. She broke the law and that made her lose Lila. But . . . But it's impossible to look at Michelle and not see how much she cares for this dog. Even when you're nearly blind, like I am. And Lila clearly loves her, too. I think that's why she was so sad for so long. She missed her person. And now that she's found her again, I'd be a real jerk to keep them apart.

"Can I come visit her sometime?" My voice is barely above a whisper when I ask.

"Sure," Michelle says. "Once she gets settled in with me I think Lila would like that."

"You promise you'll take good care of her, right? You'll give her lots of carrots and play tug with her every day?"

Michelle smiles at me, then looks back down at Lila. She's still rubbing her head. "I promise."

It ain't long after that that we leave the rescue. Lila whines about leaving Michelle, who gives her a big hug before Beth and I lead her away, but she only sulks for a little bit. By the time we get back to Beth's house, she's in a good mood again. A real good mood. She's running up and down the hallway and trying to coax Beth and me into playing tug-of-war any time we stand still for too long. I think she knows somehow that this separation ain't permanent. That we'll take her back to Michelle soon enough.

That night before bed I walk over to the desk in my room. There's a big stack of envelopes on it. All the letters Mama's sent since I got here. There's been at least one a week. Beth won't let me throw them out, but I still ain't opened a single one. Staring at the stack, I can't help but remember another stack of envelopes. Bills piled up on the table. Mama's tired sigh and the way she'd run her hands through her hair when she looked at them.

Mama's sent so many letters and called every single day, even though I ain't written back or talked to her on the phone. She ain't giving up.

Just like Michelle didn't give up on finding Lila.

Before I can talk myself out of it, I pick up the stack of letters and go to sit down on my bed. I call Lila to me and make her lie next to me while I do this. She rests her head in my lap, eyes staring up at me. Just a little bit of moral support.

And, after one long, shaky breath, I open the first envelope and stare down at my mama's familiar, big-lettered handwriting.

Chapter Twenty-Two

Shelby comes over on Monday afternoon to help me pack up Lila's things. She brings Pilot with her, which maybe wasn't the best idea, since he's real excited to be in a new house and spends most of the time just bouncing around and sniffing every nook and cranny he can find. Lila follows him, as if she's the babysitter making sure he ain't getting into too much trouble.

"Is that everything?" Shelby asks as she drops Lila's tug rope into the plastic box that sits in the middle of the living room floor.

I nod. I ain't said a whole lot since Saturday, when Beth and Lila and I got back from the rescue.

"Okay." Shelby picks up the lid and fits it onto the box. "She doesn't have much. I guess that makes sense though, since y'all only had her here for the summer." She walks over to the couch and plops down. "How are you feeling about her leaving?"

I walk over and sit down next to her, wrapping my arms around myself. "I—I ain't sure, really. I know she's gonna be happy with Michelle. It's real obvious they love each other, and I think Michelle will take care of her. But . . ."

"But you're gonna miss her," Shelby says.

"Yeah."

Shelby scoots closer and slings an arm around my shoulders, giving them a squeeze. "She's gonna miss you, too," she tells me. "And didn't you say Michelle said y'all could come by and visit Lila sometimes?"

"Yeah, but . . ."

"But it ain't the same." Shelby nods. "I know." She gives my shoulders another squeeze. "I know it don't mean much, but if you're ever just missing having a dog around, you're welcome to borrow Pilot."

It ain't even half a second after she says that that we hear a small *crash* followed by Beth hollering, "Pilot! Lila! What did y'all do?"

Shelby grimaces at me. "He might not be the best replacement, but . . ."

I can't help but laugh. It's the first time I've laughed in a couple days. "Thanks, Shelby."

"You're welcome." She pulls her arm from my shoulders and folds her hands in her lap. "I know Lila's been your best friend since you got here pretty much. But school's gonna start soon, and between me and the people I'll introduce you to there, you'll have lots of friends. We just might not be as cute and furry."

A second later, Beth walks into the living room with Lila and Pilot following close behind her. Might just be my imagination—since I ain't the best at reading expressions— but both dogs look a little guilty, if you ask me.

"Did you get all her stuff packed?" Beth asks.

I nod and wave my hand toward the plastic tub in the middle of the room.

"All right. Well, Michelle should be off work by now. I told her we'd be there by six and we still gotta pick up Vanessa, so we ought to get going."

"That's my cue." Shelby gets to her feet and grabs Pilot's leash from the hook by the door. "Say goodbye to Lila, boy."

Pilot's way of saying bye to Lila is, apparently, giving her butt one final sniff.

Shelby sighs and hooks his leash on before kneeling

down and giving Lila a scratch behind the ears. Lila wags her tail and licks her face. It's a big difference from the first time she met Shelby and Pilot, when she stayed behind a bench with her back to them.

"It was nice to meet you, Lila," Shelby says in her cooing, talking-to-a-dog voice. "You're a good girl. Have fun in your new home, okay?"

Lila pants and wags her tail.

Shelby straightens up and turns to me. "I'll see you soon, right? We can hang out before school starts."

"Yeah. Of course."

"You know," Beth says. "The dog rescue is always looking for volunteers. Hadley's gonna have a little less on her plate with Lila gone. If y'all want, I can sign you up."

Shelby's voice sounds like it's raised about three octaves when she says, "Really?" with a completely unnecessary level of excitement.

"Really. It'd give y'all a chance to hang out together if you want."

"We should do it, Hadley," Shelby says. I think she's pretty much bouncing in place now.

"We'd mostly just be refilling water dishes and cleaning out pens," I point out.

"That's fine by me," Shelby says. "We'll still get to play with dogs at least a little bit. Right, Beth?"

"Most likely, yeah."

"Hadley, please, please, *please!*" Shelby begs. And now she ain't just bouncing—she's holding on to my arm with one hand and Pilot's leash with the other. And giving both an overjoyed shake. "Let's do it. It'll be fun!"

"I ain't really a dog person."

"Nobody'll believe that anymore," Beth tells me.

I sigh. But Shelby's so excited by the prospect that I can't say no. And once Lila's gone, it probably would be a good idea to keep busy so I don't miss her constantly.

"Sure. I guess we can volunteer together."

"Yay!" Shelby exclaims. "Okay. Just call me whenever you find out when we can volunteer. Thank you, Beth!"

"I ought to be thanking you," Beth says. "The rescue is always in need of help. Can't say I've ever seen someone so excited about unpaid work, though."

"Doggy cuddles are my payment," Shelby assures her.

Before she goes, Shelby gives me a hug. I'm still sitting on the couch, so she's gotta lean down to do it. She gives good hugs. Like she really means them. It dawns on me suddenly that if it wasn't for Lila, I wouldn't have made this new friend.

A lot of things would be different if it wasn't for Lila.

Once Shelby and Pilot are gone, Beth picks up the tub of Lila's things and carries it out to her car. I get Lila leashed up. She licks my face once while I'm knelt down. I wonder if she knows we're about to say goodbye.

Beth and I don't talk during the car ride. I sit in the back seat, and Lila's in her crate next to me. We pick up Vanessa from the rescue, and during the rest of the ride, she talks to Beth about paperwork and other dogs that are being adopted soon, and I just zone out for a bit.

Michelle don't live real close—it takes about an hour to get to her place. Her little house is at the end of a long gravel driveway with a wooden fence that wraps around the yard. Beth parks the car, then turns to look back at me from the front seat.

"You ready?"

I open my mouth to answer, but no words come out.

Vanessa puts a hand on my sister's shoulder. "Why don't we give them a minute?" she suggests. "We can go let Michelle know we're here. I still need to do the home check—make sure there are no weak spots in the fence."

Beth hesitates, then nods in agreement. "Yeah, all right." She looks back at me. "Y'all take your time."

I don't do anything for a minute after Beth and Vanessa get out of the car. Not until I hear Lila shift in the crate and let out a little huff of annoyance. I turn to look at her. She's staring at me through the front slats of the crate, head tilted as she studies me.

"Do you have any idea what's about to happen?" I ask her.

Lila tilts her head to the other side.

I lean forward and open the crate. Lila wiggles her way out—it ain't easy since we're still in the back seat—but she manages to squeeze out of the carrier and up into my lap. She's way too big for this, but I don't stop her. I just wrap my arms around her thick neck.

"A lot has changed because of you, you know," I tell her. "I wouldn't have started taking mobility classes and gotten my cane if not for you. I wouldn't have met Shelby. I don't even know if I'd have left Beth's house if you didn't make me. I'd still be miserable. You helped a lot, Lila."

Lila nuzzles her face against my cheek.

"I'd like to think I made things better for you, too," I say. "If it wasn't for me, Vanessa wouldn't have put your picture up on the website. Michelle wouldn't have found you. You'd still be pouting at the rescue, ignoring everybody."

Lila begins to sniff my hair and lets out a snort.

"We both did a lot of good for each other, I guess."

Her tail thumps and she wiggles slightly, trying to get more comfortable in the small space.

I press my lips together, trying to hold back tears. "I'm glad you're gonna be happy," I whisper. "I-I'm gonna try to be happy, too. That's what you'd want, right?"

Lila gives a quiet *woof* that I take as an affirmative.

"All right." I tighten my hug again, then let my arms fall away from Lila's neck. "Well, let's go, then. Michelle's waiting on you."

I open the car door, and Lila scrambles across me to hop out. I've grabbed hold of her leash so she can't run off too quick while I climb out behind her.

Lila and I start walking toward the gate. On the other side of the fence, I can hear voices—Michelle and Vanessa and Beth, all talking and laughing. They sound excited. And beside me, Lila's tail starts wagging. She's excited, too.

I look down at her one last time, and even though I feel like I wanna cry, I give her a smile.

Then I push open the gate and introduce Lila to her new home.

Chapter
Twenty-Three

"This one is my favorite," Shelby says as she hugs Wilmer, the massive Saint Bernard mix. He laps at her face with a tongue that's almost the size of her head.

"You say that about all of them," I tell her.

"Well, I *mean it* about this one."

"You say that, too."

"I can't help it!" Shelby releases Wilmer, who lets out a loud, excited *woof!* before running off to play with some of the other dogs on the other side of the dog run. "I just *really* love dogs!"

"Really? I couldn't tell," I tease.

We've been volunteering at the dog rescue for the past week. Nearly *every day* for the past week. Beth says most volunteers just come in once or twice a week or on the weekends, but after our first day, Shelby has insisted we come in every morning to help. Well, help and play with dogs, of course.

I don't really love cleaning out the dog kennels, but doing it with Shelby makes it more interesting, at least. And it has kept me busy since Lila left. I still miss her a whole lot, but it is easier to deal with when I've got stuff to do and a friend to do it with.

It's nearly ten. Usually we don't finish until noon, when Mrs. McGraw comes by to pick Shelby and me up to take us back to our neighborhood. But today, I'm leaving early, and Beth is the one who appears at the gate of the dog run.

"Hadley?" she calls out. "You ready to go?"

I nod. My stomach gets really tight all of a sudden as my nervousness creeps up on me.

"Good," Beth says. "Shelby, I just called your dad and reminded him he'll need to pick you up today. He'll be here at noon."

"Okay," Shelby says. "Thank you, Beth." She turns to me and gives me a big hug. She's still real good at them. "Have fun today," she says. "Tell Maya and Joey I say hi. I know they don't know me, but they post really cute pictures. And their comments on your photos make them seem real nice."

"I'll tell them," I say.

"Okay. See you in a couple days!"

She lets me go. I unfold my cane and walk over to Beth, who opens the gate for me. We're quiet as we make our way around the side of the building toward her little blue car.

I ain't actually told Shelby where I'm going today. Not the whole truth of it. I ain't ready for that just yet. Seeing Joey and Maya will only be the first stop of the day. Beth and I are gonna meet them at our favorite pizza place in my old neighborhood to have a late lunch. But we've got somewhere else to go after.

It's the last Sunday before school starts on Wednesday, and Beth and I got a long trip ahead of us. We make the most of it in silence. It ain't as tense as the first long drive we took together at the start of the summer. This time, I'm glad she's here. I just don't know what to say. And I'm glad that, for once, she ain't pushing.

Joey and Maya are waiting outside the pizza place when Beth's car pulls up. They run to my door as soon as I open it and immediately engulf me in hugs.

"It's so good to see you!" Joey says.

"We've missed you so much!" Maya exclaims.

"I've missed y'all, too."

When they release me, I unfold my cane and hold it in front of me like I'm supposed to. I don't even think about it first. It's starting to become a habit now. So it ain't until there's a beat of silence that I realize it's the first time Joey and Maya have seen it in person.

If I'm nervous about that, though, I quickly realize I don't gotta be.

"Cool," Maya says. "Do we get to see how you use it, then? I've been curious."

"Sure, I guess. Though we're just going inside to eat so we probably won't be walking too much."

"Do you ever, like, trip people with it?" Joey asks.

"No. Not supposed to do that." I gotta hold back a laugh when I answer him.

"But you've thought about doing it, right?"

"Oh, definitely."

Beth comes around from her side of the car then. "Sorry. Had to answer a text. I'm Beth, Hadley's big sister. Y'all must be Joey and Maya."

"That's us," Maya says. "Also, wow, Hadley, you and your sister look a lot alike."

"You do," Joey says, and I can tell from his tone that he's

grinning. "And that's a compliment. If Hadley grows up to be half as pretty as you, Beth, she'll be a lucky girl."

Maya and me both elbow him at the same time.

"Stop flirting with my sister," I say. "She's got a girlfriend."

Beth just laughs. "Thank you, though. I do think Hadley and I look a lot alike. We take after our mama."

"Oh . . . that's right," Maya says. "You're gonna see her today, aren't you?"

I nod.

"I still can't believe she's in jail," Joey says. "How're you feeling about seeing her there?"

"I dunno."

"Well," Maya says quickly, "you don't gotta think too much about it just yet. First, you've got some pizza to eat."

"That's right," Beth says. "Oh man. Mr. Gino's Pizzeria. I haven't eaten here in so long. Is their sauce still amazing?"

"It is," Joey assures her.

"Good. Let's get some lunch, then."

We spend the next hour shoving our faces with pepper-oni pizza and talking like it'd only been a day since we'd last seen each other. I'm surprised by how easy it is. Even though we've been staying in touch more lately, I was still worried. Worried that them knowing about Mama or seeing my cane would make it feel weird. But it doesn't.

They're still Joey and Maya.

And I'm still their best friend.

Before Maya's parents come to pick her and Joey up, we make Beth take our picture so we can post it on all our socials. It's been a while since we've taken a photo together. It's long overdue.

We make promises to text and video chat as often as we can. Maya starts planning fall break and scheming so that I can come down and stay with her for a few days. And then lunch is over, and we gotta say goodbye.

"Good luck," Joey murmurs as he hugs me goodbye. "With your mama."

"Thanks," I say.

I wave as I watch them climb into Maya's parents' car and drive off.

Beth puts a hand on my shoulder. "Come on, Baby Sister," she says. "We don't wanna be late." She pauses. "Sorry. Hadley, I mean."

I shake my head. "No," I say, finally feeling okay to

acknowledge the slow thawing that's been happening in my chest for a couple months now. "Baby Sister is all right."

Beth smiles. "All right, then. Let's get going, Baby Sister."

And we get back into her little blue car.

It's right about four o'clock, according to my phone, when we pull into the parking lot and Beth cuts the engine. For a second, we both just sit there, staring out through the windshield.

"We have an hour," she tells me. "But we don't gotta stay the whole time if you don't want to."

"Okay."

I slide my hands nervously over my jeans, and little strands of dog hair cling to my palms. Silly as it sounds, realizing that none of them belong to Lila hits me with a pang of aching sadness.

Beth waits another minute before asking, "You ready, Baby Sister?"

I take a deep breath, then nod slowly.

Beth unlocks the doors and we both climb out of the car. It's still summer, so the back of my shirt and jeans feel warm and wrinkled from sitting too long. I spend more time than I need to smoothing them out, but Beth waits. When

I'm done, I unfold my cane and follow my sister across the parking lot and toward the large, block-shaped building.

We've gotta go through security as soon as we get inside. A woman in a uniform takes my cane from me for a second, since it'll set off the metal detector. She gives it back with a quiet, "Here you go, sweetheart," when we're through. I hold it tight in my right hand while Beth squeezes my left. I ain't sure if the gesture's more for her or me.

My sister leads the way down a short hallway and to a set of double doors. Another security guard opens them for us, and we step into a big, square room. A few long tables are lined up end-to-end, dividing the room in half. On one side—the side Beth and I walk in on—there are a bunch of people. Men, women, even a few other kids. All dressed in various colors. All chatting or laughing or even crying, if I'd have to guess based on the sniffling I can hear. And on the other side of the table are people in bright orange jumpsuits.

Beth stops next to two empty chairs. I don't sit down right away, though. I'm too busy looking at the woman on the other side of the table. She's got blonde hair, the same color as Beth's and mine, pulled back into a low ponytail, and she's wearing the same orange jumpsuit as everyone else on her side of the table.

And even though I'm going blind and I ain't seen her in months, I recognize her immediately.

"Hey, Hadley," she says. Her voice is a bit hoarse, and I can tell she's trying not to cry.

"Hi, Mama."

For a second, I'm overwhelmed. I think about those letters she sent, the stack of them I read all at once. They'd been full of apologies and promises that things would be better one day. But also just stories about what she was doing in jail—working in the kitchens, reading lots of books. Until now, though, all of that had been hard to imagine—Mama *actually* in jail or the future she kept assuring me of in that big, bold print.

But now I'm here, seeing her in person for the first time in months. And it all feels real. Her actually living in this place, locked away. But also that, eventually, she'll get out of here. And we'll get to be together again.

And despite everything I've said or felt all summer, looking at her, hearing her voice—I know that's all I really want.

Mama turns and looks over at my sister then. "Hi, Beth."

"Hey." I think Beth might be trying not to cry, too.

"It's good to see y'all," she says. "I . . . I've missed you. Both of you. Come on and, uh, sit down, okay?"

Beth sits down. I take a second longer, giving myself time to fold up my cane before sitting beside her, across from Mama.

There's an awkward silence for a minute, then Mama reaches across the table and takes my hand. Glancing over, I can see she's taken one of Beth's, too. My sister and I look at each other for a second, then look back at her.

"I'm sorry," she says, and she ain't bothering not to cry now. "To both of y'all. I'm . . . I'm so sorry."

"Me, too," Beth says, and now she's crying, too.

"And me, too." And, dang it, I'm crying as well.

I'd be embarrassed if I didn't get the feeling everyone in this room was far too preoccupied to notice us.

We all take a minute just to sit and look at each other before Mama focuses on me, squeezing my hand. "You start school this week, right?"

I nod.

"Sounds like you've had a busy summer," she says. "I heard there was a dog named Lila involved. And I can see you've got a shiny new cane here. Can you tell me about it?"

"I thought Beth had been filling you in on everything," I say.

"I did," Beth agrees. "Most of it."

Mama nods. "She did. But I've missed your voice, Hadley. And I wanna hear it from you. Why don't you start at the beginning. Tell me all about the adventures you've been on this summer."

So I do.

Acknowledgments

So many people (and animals) have impacted the creation of this book, and I could not be more grateful to all of them.

Thanks to my publishing team: Brianne Johnson and Allie Levick at Writers House and Jody Corbett, David Levithan, and the whole Scholastic team, specifically Baily Crawford, Josh Berlowitz, Elisabeth Ferrari, Emily Heddleson, Lizette Serrano, Erin Berger, Rachel Feld, Julia Eisler, Jana Haussmann, and Ann Marie Wong. I've been very blessed to have the most amazing people in my corner. Thank you all for believing in Hadley's story.

Thanks to my family and friends—you all are my biggest fans, my toughest critics, and always, always, always my champions. There are too many of you to name here, but you know who you are. And you know that I love you.

Thank you to all the Orientation and Mobility teachers I've had over the years, and to all the O&M teachers out there helping blind kids and adults. I don't know where I'd be today without the skills I learned from my instructors.

Thank you to Corey. I know you'll never read this (you're a dog, after all), but you've changed my life just as much as many of the people listed here. Getting a service dog was the smartest decision of my life. You've opened my heart, brought me a greater sense of independence, and inspired me to tell more stories about the amazing bond between people and animals. Thank you for being the best good girl. I'm sorry I don't give you more treats.

And, finally, thank *you*! Yes, you. My readers. None of this—none of my books—would be possible without you. Thank you!

About the Author

Kody Keplinger was born and raised in a small Kentucky town. During her senior year of high school, she wrote her debut young adult novel, which has since been adapted into a major motion picture. She is the author of many other books as well, including the middle-grade novel *The Swift Boys & Me*. Her books have landed on the *New York Times* bestseller list, the *USA Today* bestseller list, and the YALSA Top Ten Quick Picks for Reluctant Young Adult Readers list, and have been nominated for numerous awards. Kody lives in New York City, where she teaches writing workshops and continues to write books for kids and teens. You can find more about her and her books at kodykeplinger.com.